WITH A FACE OF GOLDEN PLEASURE

Copyright 2017 by Grand Mal Press. All rights reserved. Printed in the United States of America. No part of this book may be used or reproduced in any manner whatsoever without written consent except in the case of brief quotations embodied in critical articles or reviews. For information, address www.grandmalpress.com

Published by: Grand Mal Press, Forestdale, MA
www.grandmalpress.com

With a Face of Golden Pleasure,
Ryan C. Thomas, copyright 2016
Library of Congress Cataloging-in
Publication Data
Grand Mal Press
p. cm
Cover art by Grand Mal Press

This work originally appeared in the Elements of the Apocalypse *anthology from Permuted Press, 2011*

Gophers *originally appeared in the* Choose *limited edition collection from Thunderstorm Books, 2015*

First standalone edition
987654321

WITH A FACE OF GOLDEN PLEASURE

A Novella

by Ryan C. Thomas

The water understands
Civilization well;
It wets my foot, but prettily
It chills my life, but wittily,
It is not disconcerted
It is not broken-hearted
Well used, it decketh joy,
Adorneth, doubleth joy:
Ill used, it will destroy,
In perfect time and measure
With a face of golden pleasure
Elegantly destroy.

– "Water" by Ralph Waldo Emerson

DAY ONE

CHAPTER 1

Sweet Child O' Mine was playing low over the pub's speakers as Cameron came out of the bathroom, his head a little foggier than before he'd gone in. He felt like he'd just pissed all of his body's water into the gum-filled urinal. The sun was directly over the ocean, coming through the pub's beachfront window with the intensity of a fiery lance cutting through infant flesh. An air conditioner whirred in the transom over the front door, but it may as well have been a politician up there for all the useless hot air it was breathing out. The heat wave ravaging southern California was only getting worse, and the ocean waves seemed to take this as a cue to disappear. There hadn't been a swell worth talking about in over two weeks.

Cam scanned the bar. Joe was across the empty room flipping through the selections on the jukebox. Behind the counter, the tattooed bartender was talking on the pub's phone. He gave Cam an annoyed glare and plugged his free ear with his finger as Axl Rose wailed on about a girl with eyes of the bluest skies.

Cam sat at the stool in front of his beer. His musical selections queued up, Joe returned and slumped down next to him.

"They don't have Social D."

"What?" Cam asked, finishing off the remainder of his Budweiser. It tasted flatter than it had five minutes ago.

"Social D. They ain't got it. I want to hear *Ring of Fire*."

"That's Johnny Cash."

"Yeah, but the cover song is better."

"So you played Guns N' Roses instead?"

Joe wiped the sweat off his forehead with the back of his hand and finished his own beer. "I like Guns and Roses. Did like 'em anyway, before Axl went all rock star. Jesus, it's hot. You hear they're saying we might not be able to wash our cars and water our lawns and stuff. Water shortage laws."

"You don't have a lawn." Cam craned his neck to get the bartender's attention. The man was clearly in the midst of a heated argument, judging by the way he was grimacing. "And your car is a '78 Chevelle with a hole in the bottom you can see the road through. It doesn't need washing, it needs a 21-gun salute."

"Got us here, didn't it?"

"Leaving a cloud of grime behind us. What's with this bartender? He sees I'm empty. Another second I'm gonna hop over the bar and just pour one myself."

"You do that. Me, I gotta sober up and get ready for work."

"We leaving?"

"In a few."

"Cool. Can you take me back to the apartment?"

"Yeah, about that . . . um . . . "

"What?"

Joe ran his hands through his slick hair, his face suddenly aged and jaded for a man of only twenty-six. With a sigh, he looked up at Cam and said, "You know what, I will have one more beer."

Something is going on here, thought Cam. He'd seen that look in Joe's eyes before. It was the same one he got whenever he went off about quitting his job or rising gas prices or his monthly decision to be vegetarian (which only ever lasted as far as the nearest In N Out was located). It was a precursor to something Joe considered important, but was often more trivial than Cam cared to discuss.

While Joe searched for the right words to whatever it was he wanted to talk about, Cam seized the opportunity to wave at the bartender. "Hey, dude, can we get a drink down here?"

The bartender placed the phone against his chest, looked around the bar to see if anyone else had come in. When he saw that Cam and Joe were the only ones present, he said, "Hop over and get it yourself, I'm on a call." He put the phone back to his ear, spoke for a second, seemed to consider something and turned back to Cam. "Don't think you're not paying for it. I'm watching you."

"Whatever, dude." Cam hopped over, grabbed two new glasses from the small refrigerator and poured himself an Amstel Light from the tap. He snapped his fingers at Joe. "What do you want?"

"Same. On second thought, that looks foamy. Get me the Heineken."

The beer was coming out of both taps rather slowly and sudsy, which Cameron knew could be any number of problems. Normally, he would complain, but since he had carte blanche of the bar right now, he was willing to let it slide. To make matters worse, the glasses were warm, so he placed them on the bartop and went over to the ice machine near the kegs. As a bartender himself, he knew warm glasses simply meant poor management. In heat this bad there was no excuse for foamy beer and a broken glass refrigerator. Inside the ice machine all he found was a lonely baseball-sized chunk of ice. Strike three, he thought. Should he tell the bartender he needed to run the joint better? Fuck it, he thought, he wouldn't want some patron telling him the same. He'd just deal with warm, shitty beer.

As he came back around the bar to the stools Joe said, "I need you out of the apartment, Cam."

Blindsided, Cam sat down and shook his head. "What?" Was that what Joe wanted to talk about? He was kicking him out? How could he do that? It had only been two weeks. How did Joe expect him to get a place of his own in only two weeks?

"Look. I told you you could stay with me for a bit—"

"It's only been two weeks." Cam held up two fingers to illustrate how small that number was. "I'm looking."

"You said you were looking last week."

"I was."

"Bullshit. You went surfing every day."

"And I looked too."

"Where?"

"Around."

Joe shook his head. He wasn't buying it. "Around where? Give me a complex name."

"The Pines," Cam said, his voice low..

"The Pines is down the street from my apartment. I pass it every day on the way to work. It's a condo complex, so unless you suddenly got yourself a mortgage, you need to lie better."

"Then it wasn't the Pines. I forget the name."

"Seriously, Cameron—"

"Okay. Okay. I went surfing. They kept saying a swell was coming."

"Ain't no swell coming. Not today, not tomorrow. The weather is fucked up. Something about the humidity and the pressure systems and . . . "

On the jukebox, Axl Rose stopped singing and passed the microphone to Halen. Cameron laughed. "Now look who's trying to bullshit. You don't know dick about meteorology."

"But I know about living like a slob," Joe said, his attitude suddenly assertive, "and that's you. I got socks all over the damn living room, your underwear is practically in the sink, you cut your own damn hair in the bathroom two days ago and it's still all over the place. Christ, there was hair in my bed. It's like a wookie exploded in there."

"I'll clean it up."

"You take long showers, using up all the hot water. The goddamn ceiling drips on my head like it's raining when I go in there. The landlord is gonna make me pay to get rid of all the mold and—"

"So I'll stop showering."

"Look, no offense, dude, but I can't live with you anymore. You're . . . you're . . . this ain't college anymore. You gotta be responsible, which you're clearly not."

"What am I supposed to do? I can't sign a lease—is this the Sammy Hagar Van Halen?"

"Are you hearing what I'm saying?"

"Yeah. But please, Joe, I got nowhere else to go."

"That's the worst Richard Gere I ever heard, and yes, you do, you can go home."

The word drove a spike into Cam's gut. Home. Did he even have a home anymore? He hadn't spoken to Rebecca in over a week, hadn't heard his little boy's cooing in just as long, not since that last phone call when Rebecca made it clear he wasn't welcome anymore. "She told me never to come back."

"Jesus, Cam, she's still your wife. Cobalt is still your kid. You have to go back and make things right."

"You have a kid named Cobalt?" The bartender was off the phone, leaning on the bar not far away.

"Yeah," replied Cam, "and you have a crappy ice machine and foamy beer. What of it?"

"The machine is on the fritz, the water don't run for some reason. I checked it this morning. I'll check the beer in a minute. If you want to have an attitude about it, you can leave. I'm not that hard up for your seventy-five cent tips."

"He's sorry," Joe said. "His wife kicked him out of his house."

"I can see why."

"It ain't my house." Cam downed the rest of the beer in one big gulp. "It belongs to Rebecca and Scott. I'm not even on the title."

"It's still a place to live," Joe said. "Because you know what? I love you, but you can't stay with me. I'm sorry."

"You love me?"

"Not like that. Not unless you buy me dinner first."

They both chuckled. The bartender seemed unamused by it all. He'd obviously spent too many mornings serving drunk surfers to ever crack a smile again.

The music died out and the place went silent once again. Outside, seagulls squawked as they dived for the water. There were so many gulls Cam figured something large and dead must be floating near the edge of the water. Could be a seal from the La Jolla rookery. Which might mean a shark was in the area. That was all they needed. It was bad enough the waves were dead, they didn't need Jaws out there as well.

Finally, he put a ten on the bar and turned to Joe. "Okay, let me get my stuff. I'll go back and try to talk to Becky. But if she don't let me move back in, and I die in an alley somewhere—"

"People don't die in alleys in San Diego."

"People also don't choose Sammy Hagar over David Lee Roth but stranger things have happened."

"If you die in an alley you can come back as a ghost and haunt me."

"That's quite a consolation prize. Thanks for nothing."

Together, Cam and Joe ambled out of the bar and grabbed their surfboards, which they'd left standing against the wall near the door. As they headed to the car, Cam could have sworn he heard the bartender say, "Cobalt?"

CHAPTER 2

The baby had been crying way too long, and even though Rebecca loved her little boy in that selfless way only a mother can, she was about two seconds away from laying him in his crib and driving to Alaska for a moment of quiet. "Please, Cobe," she said, bouncing him in her arms as she went to the stove to see if his formula was ready, "just give me some kind of sign. Are you sick? Is it gas?"

As much as the crying was driving her mad, it was driving her even madder that she couldn't figure out why her baby was in discomfort. He hadn't cried like this since his last diaper rash, which was some three months ago. A call to the doctor resolved nothing, other than being told that crying was normal for babies, and if he wasn't hot, or spitting up, or having diarrhea, chances were he was just hungry. Either that, or sometimes the dry air can give him a headache. Keep him hydrated, the doctor had said.

Through the kitchen window, she saw Scott working on the flower garden in the front yard. How he found the strength to work half his week in the desert and then spend his one day off in more dirt planting flowers was beyond her. But then, perhaps it just gave him an excuse to get out of the house and not have to deal with his nephew's crying. Couldn't blame him for that, really.

She took the bottle from the pot on the stove, and, still holding Cobalt, dripped some on her arm. It felt right. "Here, Cobe, drink this."

Cobalt's eyes, blue as the ocean—and the source of his name—went wide as she plunged the bottle's rubber nipple into his mouth. Apparently hunger was not the source of his problem; he was still more intent on crying than eating. "Shit." Rebecca put the bottle down on the counter and moved on to plan two, which involved impressions of Yosemite Sam.

"Listen here, ya ornery varmint, I'ma givin ya till five to shut up or I'ma start shootin'. One. Two."

Ding.

Why was Scott ringing the doorbell, she wondered. He wasn't, he was still visible through the window, his arms covered in dirt, his eyes now focused on the front door where someone was waiting. Which, considering it was Tuesday at noon and the regular world was at work, could only be one person. "Jesus. Not now."

She opened the door, found Cam on the doorstep. She shut the door in his face.

"Whoa, Becky, wait." The door bounced off his foot, which he'd wedged in the jamb, and swung back open.

"Don't you come in here," she told him, bouncing Cobalt once more.

He looked back over his shoulder at Scott, judging that he was far enough away to speak openly. As if it mattered. She could see the spot on his neck where the hickey had been.

Not a hickey from her, which would be fine and amusing, but a hickey from some slut he'd met at work. Even now she could visualize him in the parking lot after locking up the bar. Could see some ugly bitch sucking on his neck. Their hands groping one another. It made the hairs on her arm stand up. If she ever found out who the whore was she'd kill her.

Seeing he was a safe distance from Scott, he turned back to her. "C'mon Becky, let's talk. Please?"

"I got nothing to say to you, Cam. Maybe your girlfriend will talk to you. Or fuck you. Or whatever else you do with her."

"She's not my girlfriend. It was a one-time thing. I don't even know her name."

"Oh, great, that makes it so much better! Goodbye."

"Wait!" Cam stepped into the house.

Through the door, Rebecca saw Scott start toward the house. She shook her head no and he got the message. He bent down and concentrated on his flower bulbs. She scowled at Cam. "I said not to come in."

"Sorry. Look, I just...I miss you. I miss Cobe. Can I hold him?"

As much as she was pissed at Cam for cheating on her, she couldn't deny him the right to hold his child. And right now, she could use a break from the baby's crying. It went against her better judgment, but she nodded and handed Cobalt over to him.

As soon as Cam held Cobalt to his chest the baby stopped crying. Great, she thought, way to mock me, God.

"Hey, Cobe, Daddy missed you, buddy." The baby

smiled and gurgled, a picture-perfect moment from another time. Another time when adultery had been just a word in a Charlton Heston film during which she'd fallen asleep. Cam touched Cobalt's cheek. "He been crying? His face is all puffy."

"Nonstop," she replied. "I don't know what's wrong."

"You give him a bottle?"

"No, I gave him thumb tacks and bleach and sat him on broken glass."

"Point taken. But hey, he ain't crying now."

That was a blessing, she thought. It might even be worth it to have Cam stay for a little bit until the baby fell asleep. Maybe Cam would fall asleep too and she could smother him with a pillow or something, get back at him for ruining her life.

Lucky for him she didn't watch enough *CSI* to pull it off. "Come sit so you don't drop him," she said.

Wisely, Cam decided not to rebut to the snide comment and carried the baby over to the living room couch. Baby blankets and rattles covered the cushions. On the television, *Sesame Street* was on, the volume turned low. Rebecca went into the kitchen, got the bottle and handed it to him, just in case Cobe would eat.

Sighing, she sat in the recliner next to Cam and felt her back ache.

"How have you been?" he asked her, lightly rocking Cobalt in his arms.

"Why do you care?"

"Because you're my wife and I love—"

"Don't say it, Cam. Don't you dare say that in front

of your son. If you loved me, you would have come home and gotten in bed with *me*. Not some slut you met at the bar."

"I made a mistake, Becky. I know that now. I can't take it back but I can guarantee it don't happen again. I want to come back home to you and Cobe."

The way he spoke sounded sincere, but she couldn't trust him now. Not after what he'd done to her, how much he'd hurt and humiliated her.

"Joe kicked me out," he said, his eyes locked on the baby's.

Was he afraid to look at her, she wondered. Did he actually think she would feel sorry for him? Would he even *be* here if Joe had let him stay? She was so pissed she didn't even know what to say.

Cobalt stared back at his daddy with wonder, like he'd forgotten who Cam was. That was something she didn't want her baby to go through. It wasn't the baby's fault his daddy was a whore; he deserved to have his father around. She knew too well the pain that came with losing a father. And a mother.

The images of the accident flashed through her mind, sadness creeping up on her again. She looked around the house, taking in the mess from the baby and thought of how hard it would be to raise Cobalt in a small apartment in one of the cheap beach towns. The house provided so much for her and the baby. Still, she'd give up the house in a heartbeat if she could get her parents back.

"I'm sorry," she said, though it was more just something to say than an actual truth. "Maybe you could find a room somewhere."

"C'mon, Becky, this is killing me. I screwed up, I get it, just give me a chance. It was just one time. Don't you want to be a family again?"

Her answer was quick and firm. "No."

The door opened and Scott came in, his shirt dirty with soil, some grass sticking in his hair. He respectfully ignored the conversation in the living room and poured himself a glass of water from the kitchen tap. Cam didn't say anything, obviously not wanting Scott to overhear their conversation. He made cooing sounds to Cobalt. The baby's eyes were growing heavy and Rebecca was at least thankful for that.

Scott came back from the kitchen with a glass of cloudy water. "You mess with the faucet?"

"No," Rebecca replied.

"Coming out real slow and aerated."

Rebecca hated it when he used scientific words around her; it made her feel stupid. It was one thing for her brother to sound scholarly in front of his scientist friends, but in front of her, she wished he'd just speak in layman's terms.

"Too much oxygen," he said, seeing the annoyance in her face.

"I know." She actually did know; she had heard Scott say it before.

"Well, maybe the pipes got clogged or something. I'll check them in a few." As an afterthought, he nodded to Cameron, said, "Cam," and went back outside.

On the television, Bert and Ernie were arguing about something, and Rebecca couldn't help but notice the parallel. "Cobe's asleep. Time for you to go."

"So no deal. I can't come back."

"No."

"Then when?"

"When you take back what you did."

"How do I do that, invent a time machine?"

"You figure it out. Just leave Cobe on the couch, I'll put him in his crib in a minute."

Rising from the chair, she went to the front door and opened it, motioned for him to leave. Cam's face was long as he slowly got up from beside his sleeping baby boy and reluctantly left the place he'd called home just two weeks ago. "Where do I go?" he asked her.

He looked genuinely sad and lost, and it killed her that she could still feel so much love for him despite what he'd done. Part of her wanted to grab him, pull him inside and just turn back time to when they were happy. Tell him he could stay here, but the part of her that knew his words were lies made her want to tell him exactly where he could go.

He looked in her eyes. "I love—"

The door cut him off .

CHAPTER 3

Since the wildfires two years ago, Scott had been planning on planting succulents around the house in the event of a repeat blaze. To be more exact, he'd been planning on helping his father plant them.

Then the accident happened last year.

Now, he could at least honor the old man's memory and do what he'd been meaning to do before the collision. More importantly, the house was half his now and he didn't want to see his childhood home go up in flames if he could help it.

Cam was still inside with his sister, and he was amazed she'd let him in for this long. The things she said she'd do to Cam if he ever came back were so evil the devil would be afraid of her. Hell hath no fury…

"Whatcha planting?"

Scott looked up and saw Cam standing over him; he hadn't heard him come out. "Some aloe, ice plant, some other things." He motioned toward the door with his head. "So, how'd it go?"

"She said I can't come back. I don't know what to do. I have nowhere to stay."

"That's a tough one." Scott stood up and brushed dirt off his clothes. "She doesn't let things go very easily. I stole one of her dolls when I was about fifteen—she was around ten—stole it for a science experiment and she still hasn't forgiven me. I melted its face off with toothpaste—"

"Toothpaste? How do you do that?"

"Never mind. Too long to explain. Point is, just the other day she was online buying a doll for Cobe and she saw one that reminded her of it. Gave me a hard time all day."

"That was just a doll, this was . . . "

"Yeah, I know. You cheated on her. Dumb move."

"You mad at me?"

Sure, he was mad at Cam. Who wouldn't be mad at someone who had a baby with their sister and then cheated on her? Not to mention the fact Cam and Becky were living in the house with him, since it was legally half hers now. He'd been present when Cam came home with the hickey. He had seen his sister's face and the hurt that seized her when Cam finally confessed. "Cam, I like you. I really do. But you're kind of on your own here."

"C'mon, Scott. You're smart, you must know what she wants."

"What she wants? Jesus. I'm not old enough to be your father, Cam, but I am your brother-in-law, so let me give you some friendly advice. It's time to grow up."

"I am grown up. Dress myself and everything."

"You own anything besides rock t-shirts and sandals?"

"Don't forget the shorts. And underwear. Actually, scratch that, I'm commando today. I think I got some underwear in the trunk of my car, though."

"Quit joking around. You got a kid in there and he

needs to be raised. He needs food and clothes and toys at Christmas. He needs someone to teach him how to surf when he gets older. Yeah, I thought that would get through to you. You could start by getting a real job."

"You expect me to suddenly become CEO of some company overnight. Shit, maybe this is for the best. She hates me anyway."

The grass had become a crispy yellow. Scott wished he could run the sprinkler, but he'd heard they were passing a water ban. If it didn't rain soon he might as well just pave the yard and put in a basketball court. He kicked at the burnt lawn as he thought about what to tell Cam. "She still loves you, you know. She misses you. Don't get me wrong, she's liable to kill you just the same, but I know she misses you because I can hear her crying at night. Considering that I have to be at the dig site so much, she could use help with the baby. So, I'm going to help you out, but do me a favor and don't say anything to her. Give me a couple days to talk to her. In the meantime . . . " He took a set of keys from his shorts pocket and handed them over. "There's a trailer set up at Basin Springs."

"That place where everybody rides their dirt bikes?"

"Yeah. I'm studying the ground sediment to see if it's an aquifer." Cameron looked lost, so he explained it as quickly as he could. "If there's water underground they're gonna put a pump in and see if they can irrigate the surrounding farms. This drought is killing everything. Anyway, you can stay in Trailer Three. That one's mine. Wait until night and then go by. Just be gone before six when the team shows up."

"Six?! In the morning?!"

"I'm trying to help you out here, Cam. Help me out, okay?"

Cam nodded and took the keys.

After he was gone, Scott looked at the sky. He'd never spoken to the sky before the accident, but he'd done it a few times since, each time feeling like he was dishonoring everything he believed about science and evolution. Thinking that maybe, just maybe, someone might be listening . . . he could see why his parents had made him go to church when he was younger. It was something to hold onto when there was nothing but pain. It didn't mean he bought into any of it, but he could understand its void-filling appeal more now than he did a year ago. Still, science was truth, God was wishful thinking. Which is why he flushed with embarrassment as he began to speak. "Dad, she needs him. So any help you can give is appreciated. I know men like Cam, and some of them can learn. I think maybe he's realizing how much he needs her, too. And besides, I'm through changing diapers. I swear that baby waits for me to get near him so he can kill me with a Gerber's uppercut."

When he bent down to continue planting the succulents, he saw the glass of water he'd been drinking was almost empty. That was strange. Had he spilled some without noticing?

CHAPTER 4

Cam found the series of trailers at the end of a dirt path that ran through Basin Springs. They were small and old, built sometime in the seventies, coated in desert dust. A single yellow bulb was strung up outside the door of Trailer Three. Right now it was attracting a family of winged insects large enough eat a dog. Inside the trailer was even worse. Jam-packed with geological equipment from the University, the only place to sit down was on a small cot at the back. At least Scott had had the good sense to put in a small fridge and old television set. Hopefully the bathroom had enough legroom for him to do any business that might come up.

Basin Springs was anything but a spring, having dried up back before the first world war. Now it was just a big flat plain of desert and rock with the occasional dead reptile littering the ground for decoration. Foothills rose around it, creating the actual walls of the basin, and providing a home for coyotes that, even now, were barking for food. It was a good half hour north of Escondido in the middle of nowhere and a few miles from the river.

He turned the television on and threw himself down on the bed, thinking about what Scott had said to him. He'd said he didn't want to act like Cam's dad but he sure as hell sounded like it. It was understandable to a degree, what with Rebecca and Scott's family having been killed in the car accident last year. Scott saw himself as the man of the house now, since he was the oldest. But Scott didn't have a baby or a wife so what did he really know about being an adult? All Scott did was play with rocks all day.

Besides, bartending wasn't such a bad job. He probably made just as much as Scott at the end of the day. How much could a rock scientist really make?

He found a beer in the fridge.

"Look at you, Scotty, keeping booze at work. Maybe you're not the geek I thought you were." He popped the cap and, realizing the bottle felt light, held it up in the glow of the television. "What is this, half drunk or something?"

The bottle's cap had been tight, but the beer inside was half gone. Could be Scott replaced the cap, or could be that the bottling plant had screwed up. Jeez, was he going to get a beer today that wasn't flat, sudsy or half gone? "Beggars can't be choosers." He drank it down. To his surprise, it wasn't flat.

On the television, a man on the news was talking about the drought. The map behind him showed California covered with a large graphic that said: 207 days. That must be how long it had been since it rained in the state. The map cut to a picture of the entire country and each state contained a number not far from California's. The weatherman said something about the drought affecting crops in the Midwest.

"Get to the surf report already, you toupee-wearing mongoloid."

The camera cut to the desk anchor and flashed a picture of the mayor in the upper right hand corner of the screen. "Mayor Coleman issued a water ban today. Anyone found watering the lawn, washing the car, filling the pool, or using water excessively during daylight hours will be fined. California is now the twelfth state to issue a water ban. In a related story, city officials are concerned that the reservoir has already dropped below a safe level. The city is currently investigating the possibility of piping in water from Washington..."

"Great," Cam said to the television. "Now what about a fucking swell? Tell me there's gonna be a swell."

The man said nothing about waves. Instead, they cut to a story about trees dying in the park.

Done with his beer, Cam flipped stations. There was no cable out here so he was limited to whatever the set could pick up with its antenna, which wasn't much. A lot of stations from Mexcio and the few local networks. He settled on a sitcom involving a low-income family that thought jokes about school recitals were funny. It reminded him of Becky and Cobe and he found his thoughts drifting back to Scott's words. Maybe it was time to move on from bartending. It's not like he had medical benefits or anything, which the baby damn well needed. The money from Becky's parent's death was bound to dry up soon, too (thank God her father had a premium life insurance plan). So much of his income depended on getting a good shift on a weekend, it wasn't very stable.

He dialed Joe on his cell phone. Joe picked up right away but didn't say anything.

"Hey, Joe."

"You back at home?"

"No, I'm in trailer in Basin Springs."

"You're kidding."

"I wish. And to make it worse, I'm stuck watching some show called *Family Fruit.*"

"I love that show. The chick who plays the daughter is hot. Sometimes you can see her nipples through her shirt."

"You can see my nipples through my shirt and it never makes you horny."

"Yeah it does. Why do you think I go surfing with you? I was planning on slicing a vag in your taint so I could make you my woman."

"Gross."

Joe laughed.

Cam did too, then got pensive. "Seriously, your dad still looking for people to work?"

"Sure. You telling me you want to build fences now?"

"No. But I think I got a good chance of getting Becky back if I can get a job with benefits. Would he give 'em to me?"

"After three months, I think. There's a probationary period."

"Think you can talk to your dad?"

"I can talk to him. But if you flake out and go surfing or something, I'm gonna—"

"What? Kick me out of your place? Too late."

"Just be on time. I'll call him and tell him you're coming. Don't fuck off on this."

When Cameron was done talking to Joe, he dialed Becky. Scott picked up instead. He asked to talk to her but she wanted nothing to do with him. So he asked Scott to relay a message to her. "I've got an interview at SP Fence tomorrow. Tell Becky I'm changing. Oh, and you shouldn't put half finished beer in the fridge. It don't keep."

CHAPTER 5

"All I'm saying is Cobe is going to need him around." Scott put the plates from their dinner in the sink while Rebecca removed Cobalt from his high chair. He laid the glasses on top of the plates, wondering why there had barely been enough milk for dinner; they'd just bought that gallon a couple days ago.

"No, what you're saying is that it's okay for men to cheat on women because we're too frail and need a big strong man around. Bullshit. He totally disrespected me, Scott."

The tap was worse than this afternoon; hardly any water was coming out now at all. If the dirty dishes sat out all night they'd have flies in the morning. "Shit, this faucet is really busted. Where was I? Oh . . . no, what I'm saying is, yes he screwed up, in a big way, but he wants to make good so, you know, maybe you start slow and—"

"Screwed up? He shoved his dick inside another girl. See what happened when he did that to me?" She held Cobalt up to make a point. The baby started crying once again, and Scott could see Becky sigh. Cobe had been crying ever since he'd woken up and found Cam gone.

"I know. He deserves a punch in the head. And I certainly don't condone his actions. But . . . just consider it," he said. "Maybe you could go to counseling. Hell, you could certainly use it to your advantage. He'll probably do anything you want if you let him back. And like I said, think about Cobe here, about him growing up in a broken home."

"You really sound like you're okay with what he did. Don't you care about me?"

Exasperated with the faucet, he walked over to her and took Cobalt from her arms. He kissed her on the forehead. "I love you, Beck. Believe me, I wouldn't say any of this if I thought Cam hadn't just made a stupid, stupid error. He loves you, I can see it in his eyes."

"That's very romantic," she said mockingly.

"Why don't you go rest and I'll sit with Cobe and watch *Telletubies* or something."

"Fine . . . the resting part, not the Cam part. Make him a bottle while you're at it. Use the bottled water in the fridge so he doesn't grow a third ear or something." With an evident moan of relief, Rebecca walked to her room and turned on her TV.

"Come with Uncle Scott," Scott said, walking to the kitchen with the baby, thinking how strange it sounded to be called Uncle. It made him feel old. He bent down with Cobalt in his arms and looked through the fridge for the gallon of water he'd bought yesterday. It was nearly empty, hardly enough for even half a bottle for the baby.

Strange.

It usually took three or four days for Becky to go through a gallon.

DAY TWO

CHAPTER 6

Cam was up at six, thanks to the alarm on his cell phone, but the people from the University were already there. He could hear them talking outside the trailers, wondering whose car was parked near Trailer Three. What really caught his attention though was the guy saying something about bizarre stuff going on at the beach.

Was it a swell?

Joe's father wasn't expecting him until seven-thirty, so maybe he had time to hit the nearest break and check it out. He threw his clothes on so fast most of it went on backwards, and ran out of the trailer.

"Who are you?" asked a guy carrying some long poles over to where a small aquifer pump sat in the ground.

"I'm Cam, Scott's brother-in-law."

"Ah, the one who got caught cheating."

So, Cam thought, Scott was a gossip as much as a scientist. "I didn't get caught, I confessed. I do have a conscience, you know. Why the hell am I explaining this to you?"

"I don't know but I think your shorts are backwards."

"Is he here?"

"Scott? Not yet, said he was feeding the baby and then coming in."

There was little else that could make Cam feel as shitty as knowing someone else was taking care of his kid. He missed Cobe; the baby was a part of adulthood Cam was surprisingly happy about. "Tell him I was gone before you got here." The man nodded but Cam doubted his reliability. He got in his car, the surfboard still strapped to the roof, and headed west.

When he got to the beach, he could tell something was definitely going on, but it had nothing to do with a swell. Trucks from a handful of government agencies were parked in the lot, and men in Hazmat suits were running about carrying large drums. What the hell was going on? Someone spill chemicals into the water?

"Beach is closed," a man in a blue Parks and Recreation jacket told him when he got out of the car.

"What do you mean closed?"

"Well, you know when you go someplace and the doors are open and you go in. Imagine the opposite of that. If you're still confused, I can have someone explain it to you in a jail cell."

Cam spotted the police cars parked nearby; the cops were talking to some other surfers who were also looking toward the water. "Get a life," he told the guy, and left.

He drove south on the 5 for ten minutes and pulled off into a rest area overlooking the water. Several cars were already there, and people were taking video of the beach. When he got out, he saw what was causing such a stir. He drew in a sharp breath. Suddenly it felt like he was waking from a dream, still half asleep and trying to make sense of his surroundings. As understanding sank in, the hairs on the back of his neck rose.

The water had receded some quarter of a mile out to sea, as if the ocean were draining down a hole out in the middle somewhere. Dead fish and crabs littered the edge of the beach where the waves used to crash on the shore. Birds swooped in and scooped them up by the thousands. The water was eerily calm, barely moving at all.

A small path cut down the cliff to the sand below. People were walking down, drawn to the beach like magnets. There weren't any police or government agents milling around here, nor did he see them down below. He hurried to the path with an insatiable need to know what was going on burning inside him. A couple of times he almost fell as he descended but held on by grabbing the crabgrass. He was lucky it held him, as most of it was dead or dying. In fact, there was hardly anything green around at all.

On the beach, he couldn't believe his eyes. The sand, once covered with lapping waves, was littered with a million different kinds of crustaceans and marine plant life, all dead. They crunched under his sandals as he walked. A tall man with a bucket was walking out as far as the new water line, collecting oysters and mussels, most likely for dinner.

"What the hell is going on?" he asked himself, catching the attention of a nearby man in a bathing suit.

"Beats me. Came down for my morning swim and

found it like this. It's like the water just disappeared or something. Them fish is all half dried up, too. You know you got your shirt on backwards?"

Bending down, Cam picked up a tiny skipjack and felt its brittle, dry skin, saw its chalky, sunken eyes. Fish were supposed to be slimy, that much he knew. This was all wrong.

CHAPTER 7

"Where are my keys?" Scott frantically raced through the kitchen. At the table, Cobalt was playing with his rubber baby spoon. Rebecca was fiddling with the faucets at the sink and was clearly not listening to him. "Beck, my keys? You see 'em?"

"What? Oh, um, Cobe has them. He was playing with them."

"I'm thinking he had an accomplice," he said as he lifted the keys from Cobalt's lap. The baby reached up for them so Scott gave them a quick jiggle before putting them in his pocket.

"I thought you were gonna fix this?" Rebecca kept turning the spigot, getting no response.

"I tried. I'm gonna have to call a plumber. Look I gotta run, the guys at the site just called and something is up. They're all freaking out."

"What's up is I can't take a shower and Cobe needs formula and we're out of bottled water."

"I fed him, he'll survive until you can get to the store. Think about what I said, about Cam, okay?" Scott grabbed a granola bar from the cupboard and ran out the front door.

Frustrated with the plumbing, Rebecca sat down at the table next to Cobalt. The baby was content to stare back at her, finding something of interest in her eyes.

She stuck her tongue out at him and smiled when he giggled. For some reason his giggle became a cry, and then a wail. She wanted to bang her head against the wall.

"Shh. Come on, Cobe, just five minutes without crying. Please?" He's probably just thirsty, she thought, God knew she was and Scott hadn't even made any coffee this morning. Inside the fridge she took out the carton of orange juice, scowled when she found it empty. The milk was also empty, as was the pitcher of iced tea she'd made a couple days ago, nothing but dried tea stuck to the sides. "Jesus, Scott, you gonna drink everything?"

Then she saw the beers. Tentatively, she picked one off the shelf and held it up to the light coming through the kitchen window.

The bottle was sealed, but it was empty.

They were all empty.

"What the hell—"

Ding.

It was the front door. Through the window she saw Cam's clunker in the driveway. Scott had told her Cam was interviewing for a job this morning, something about manual labor for Joe Renton's Dad. Leave it to him to goof off and forget about the appointment. Jesus, he was such a fuck up!

Anger welled up in her and she forgot all about the empty beer bottle as she stormed to the door, Cobalt still crying at the table. She flung the door wide and laid into him. "Thought you were getting a job today? Or did you go surfing?"

"Can't." He stepped inside without her permission. "Something's wrong with the ocean."

"Nothing's wrong with the ocean. Sometimes it's just calm."

"It ain't the waves. The water's all screwy. It's . . . it's disappearing or something. Why are you drinking a beer this early in the morning?"

She looked at the bottle in her hand and considered what he was telling her about the water disappearing, then remembered he should be at work and not playing environmentalist at the beach. "I'm not drinking. Scott must have drunk it and put it back."

"He did that in the trailer too. He got something against throwing bottles away?"

"You didn't answer my question. I thought you had an interview today?"

"I did, I missed it. But--"

"I can't believe this! You know, Scott spent all night trying to convince me to give you a second shot. He said you were getting a good job with benefits. But instead you're at the beach. Fuck!" The bottle made a hollow *thunk* as it hit him square in the chest. It fell to the floor, bounced once, and rolled toward the couch. She immediately felt bad for losing control, but the whole cheating thing kept her from apologizing.

"Okay, that fucking hurt," he said rubbing his chest. "But I don't think you understand, there's all these cops and guys in special suits at the beach. I'm telling you, I think someone put chemicals in the water or something. What if it's terrorists?"

Hadn't Scott said something about the guys at the

dig site freaking out about something? Cam was lazy and rarely made smart decisions but he wasn't one to give into paranoia. Could there really be something going on?

No, she decided, Scott would have told her if it was something serious. His scientist friends always knew what was going on, and if there was a terrorist plot afoot they certainly wouldn't have asked him to come to work. And somebody would have called by now, even if it was just her aunt in Ohio.

"It ain't terrorists, Cam. Only terrorist you're about to see is me if Cobe doesn't get some water for his bottle so I can stop him from screaming all day."

"He's still crying?"

"He needs formula. Do me a favor, since you're not at work . . . " She let the remark linger until he rolled his eyes. "Go to the store and buy some gallons of water."

"Now?"

"Yes, now. Your son needs his bottle. Go."

"All right. Stop yelling. All you do is yell."

"All you do is screw up, you should be used to it."

"I came to check on you, least you could do--"

"I'm not afraid of the ocean, Cam, I'm afraid that Cobe is hungry. Please go get some fucking water. And fix your clothes. You look like a fucking mental patient." She slammed the door on him, leaned against the hard wood until she heard his car engine start and the car pull down the driveway.

She fought back tears.

CHAPTER 8

It didn't take a scientist to see something was wrong at the site. People were frantically running about like they were covered in fire ants, shouting orders to everyone and no one in particular. Jogging past the trailers to the water pump that rose from the dusty ground, Scott saw Professor Martin wave him over.

"Hey, Jack," Scott said, drawing up into the confusion. It still felt a little strange to call his old teacher by his first name, but they were colleagues now and it would be silly to call him Mr. Martin. "What's the matter?"

"Scott, c'mere and look at this. We're positive we located the aquifer, right?"

"Yeah. Pretty sure."

A lanky researcher in a White Stripes t-shirt ran up and blocked their path. "Excuse me, Professor Martin?"

"Yes, Shaun?" Jack looked at the empty bottle of water in the man's hand.

The man was Shaun Bonn, a graduate student who was new to the crew. Scott knew little about him, other than he was an intelligent, driven guy, and could recite the lyrics to any song ever recorded. "Professor, sorry to interrupt, but someone dumped all the water out of the bottles in the fridges. Could have been that guy that stayed here last night? It's gonna be hot today . . . "

Scott knew he was referring to Cam. Six in the

morning was an unrealistic thing to ask a guy like Cam to honor. Better to get it out there than hide it. "That was my brother-in-law. I'll make him buy new—"

"No, that's okay," Jack said. "Thanks, Shaun. I'll deal with it in a moment." He motioned for Scott to follow him to the pump once again.

"Really," Scott said, "Cam shouldn't have done that. He's going through a hard time and—"

"I don't think Cam did anything, Scott. Something is going on with the water here. Look at this and tell me what you think."

They'd arrived at the pump head, a cylindrical device about the size of an oil drum, with a long tube that ran down into the ground some three hundred feet. Yesterday there had been a modicum of moisture in the collection bin; there was nothing today. It could be that there wasn't much to begin with, but Scott was pretty sure the aquifer was there. The basin used to be filled with water in the late 1800s, and the La Dorma River ran just two miles south of here toward the Pacific.

"I don't get it," he said. "Where's the water?"

Jack took off his baseball hat, stared at the sun and said, "That's what I want to know."

CHAPTER 9

The supermarket was quiet this early on a Monday morning, nothing but a handful of the elderly comparing notes on soup can labels. The downside was that there was only one checkout register open, and if Cam got stuck behind any of these one-foot-in-the-gravers, he knew he'd be here all day while they counted out all their coupons. He didn't care much for the elderly, the way they smelled like onions and rubber sheets, and shrank to the size of hobbits. They were stranger than babies.

The juice aisle seemed to be of particular interest to three of the nearly-dead. They stood in a tight knot talking to one of the stock boys, who was replying to them the way Cam talked to Cobalt.

"Must be a bad shipment, ma'am," he was saying. "See? Just a bad shipment. I don't know what to tell you. It's all like this."

The juices and other drinks on the shelf were empty, Cam saw.

"But I'm thirsty," pleaded a little old lady of at least eighty.

Shit, Cam was thirsty too. He hadn't eaten breakfast, and aside from a burrito and a very syrupy Coke from a taco stand last night, he hadn't put anything into his system in about ten hours.

It was a moot point to ask the stockboy what was going on with the water, but he did it anyway.

"Why is everything empty?"

"Why is the sky blue? Why do birds fly? Why do I hate this frigging job more and more every day? Enquiring minds want to know." The stockboy, his smart-ass remark hanging heavy in the air, finally threw his hands up and told everyone to wait while he got the manager.

"This one has a little juice in it." One of the old men lifted up a bottle of apple juice that was three quarters of the way empty. Looking around the shelf, Cam could see a few bottles still had liquid in them, but not a lot.

When the manager arrived, he looked exasperated. "Hi, folks, I wish I could tell you what was going on here, but unless someone broke in last night and decided to play a prank I have no answers for you. I've been on the phone with my distro people all morning. Give me a few hours to straighten it out and get some shipments in. Maybe try back around four. Okay?"

"How does someone empty all the liquid and then seal up every bottle again? Cam asked.

"Like I said," the manager replied, "give me some time to figure it out. In the meantime, here are some coupons for cereals." The elderly patrons took the coupons, happy with their deal, and went to find the Mueslix.

As the stockboy and manager headed to the storeroom, Cam overheard one of them say the water was off in the whole building.

No water, he thought. Hazmat teams at the beach, empty beer, no juice.

Damn it, he was getting pretty thirsty. He grabbed a bottle of water that had about two cups left in it, paid full price for it, and left.

Before he drove back to see Becky, he stopped at a series of convenience stores. Everyone told the same story: someone had dumped out all the juice, water, soda, milk, and any other liquid in the store. The odds that some hoodlums were sneaking around town emptying every container in every store were beyond unbelievable. Not to mention that none of the stores had working plumbing. No way hoodlums could pull that off without someone noticing; they'd have to mess with the pipes under the streets.

He managed to find three more bottles that had some water left in them. Once he was in the car, he poured all the water into one jug. Some of it spilled down the side, but he was able to transfer the brunt of it without much loss. It wasn't much, but combined it was about a half a gallon. He set the bottle down and wrapped his hands around the steering wheel, noticing how they left streaks of water on the leather. Immediately, it began to recede. Not from the outside edges in, like a puddle of water should, but from everywhere at once. It was gone in seconds. Too fast, Cam thought. Sure, it was a hot day, but years of surfing told him water didn't dry that quickly. Playing with the thought, he remembered the water he'd spilled down the outside of the jug. He wanted to watch it evaporate again. But when he rubbed his hand against the jug's exterior, it was dry. Bone dry. He licked his finger and rubbed it on the dash board. The saliva streak disappeared quickly. "You've got to be kidding me."

He snatched the naked lady pen he kept in the visor, picked up the jug and drew a line across it, marking the water level.

When he pulled into the driveway at Becky's house five minutes later, the line sat about a quarter inch above the water. "What the fuck?"

It was disappearing.

Fuck knocking, he thought as he crashed through the front door calling for Becky. "Beck! Beck!"

"What? Jesus, don't yell, Cobe just stopped crying." She came out of the bathroom brushing her teeth. From the look of her rat-nest hair she hadn't taken a shower yet, and Cam had a sneaking suspicion why.

"You using water?" he asked her, already knowing the answer.

"No. Pipes are broken, remember?" She pointed to the gallon of water in his hand. "What the hell is that? You drank it already!"

"No I didn't. Remember when I said the ocean was all screwy. Well, watch this." He put the jug down on the table and grabbed a pen from the counter, marked off the water line again.

"Cam, I have shit I need to do. All I asked was that you get some water. A full bottle and you come back—"

She was going to drive him mad if she didn't just stop bitching for a second and listen to him. Okay, he'd cheated on her, he got it, but this was a little more serious than adultery in the 2000s. This was catastrophic, this was something out of the movies, this was nucking futs to the nth degree. Frustrated and past the point of concern, he grabbed her shoulders and forcibly brought her to the water. "Becky, you can hit me in a second for that move, but before you do . . . Watch. The. Fucking. Water. Please!"

That shut her up, but boy did she look pissed. No doubt she was going to take him up on his offer of pugilism, probably throw another beer bottle at him. Still, she bent over and looked at the water, eager to tell him he was an idiot.

"Keep watching," he said, "just wait."

Finally, the toothbrush fell from her mouth and landed on the floor, sending bits of toothpaste all over Cam's shorts. "How'd you do that?" she asked. "How'd you make the line move?"

"The line didn't move. The water is disappearing."

For the next couple minutes Becky was silent, perhaps trying to figure out if this was a trick. She looked at the faucet again, then at the fridge, and understanding sank in. "But how? How can it just go away?"

"No fucking clue," Cam responded. "But I know this much, seeing drunk people all the time, dehydrated and puking . . . you need water to live."

She quickly caught the meaning of his words, looked at him and whispered, "Oh, my God. Cobe."

CHAPTER 10

Noon came quickly for Scott and his crew. The day was growing hotter by the minute, the rocks and dirt almost painful to touch, and they still didn't have any water. Not that they were far away from civilization or anything, but it was going to get real uncomfortable in a few hours if someone didn't make a run to the store soon.

What was even more concerning, though, was the new issue with the aquifer. Scott had spent weeks measuring the ground, testing the rock underneath, drilling down into the water that was trapped beneath the saturated zone. It was water that had been here for ages, constantly replenished by the nearby river and sinking fog during cold nights. Whether it was enough to be economically feasible to use for irrigation was still undetermined, but there was no way it should have vanished.

"Come on, guys, put your backs into it," Scott shouted. Around him, the team of graduate students and city workers peeled back layers of the desert bedrock, exposing the interior flesh of the earth. It was dry, dead, gray, the epitome of lifelessness. Scott knew they should have hit wet clay by now, but there was nothing, no sign that water ever existed under the surface.

"I can't believe this. We're gonna lose the grant." Scott threw a rock into the sky like a man intent on shattering the clouds.

"Just the opposite," Jack said. "Disappearing aquifer needs to be studied, wouldn't you think? I wouldn't worry about money. What I'd worry about is what that guy over there is doing to the pump."

Scott ran over and steered the man away from the pressure valves he was adjusting. "Whoa! Whoa, buddy, too hot. See, you're running this too hot, that's why the needle is in the red."

The worker, slick with sweat, shrugged and walked away.

Everyone was getting too sweaty and irritable to do things correctly; the bottled water situation needed to be solved pronto.

"Jack," Scott said, taking out his car keys, "I'm going to get water. We'll all start hallucinating in a minute unless we hydrate ourselves."

"Don't bother," Jack replied, "I sent that Shaun kid. He already came back."

"Then where's the water?"

"Kid said everything at the store was either empty or damn near close. Scott, we need to talk."

Jack's tone was now serious, the kind of serious where people get fired or transferred or told their wife has been having an affair. It was never a tone you wanted to hear from someone higher up than you. "What's going on?"

"Not here. Let's go in the trailer."

When they got to the trailer, Jack sat on the cot and

turned on the television. A reporter was standing in a beach parking lot, pointing at the ocean, shaking his head like he was confused. Men in Hazmat suits were running around in the background.

"What's that all about?" Scott asked. It looked like Mann's Beach, only a few miles from where they were now. "Someone dump hospital waste or something?"

Instead of answering the question, Jack checked his watch and noted the time. "Get me a beer, Scott."

Now Scott knew something was up: Jack didn't drink beer until the end of the work day. Jack didn't do anything that could be considered rebellious. Jack was Jack, geological professor extraordinaire, always the example of professional academia.

What Scott saw inside the fridge stopped him cold. "The beer is all gone," he said.

"I know," Jack replied.

"But how—"

Jack pointed to the TV, the way he used to point to the board in class.

Together they looked at the television, listening for the first time to what the reporter was saying.

" . . . water's disappearance has city and university officials baffled. We have received word that the President is being briefed on the situation . . . "

"The water at my house wasn't running this morning," Jack said. "The juice was nearly all gone. I grabbed an apple on the way out. It was dry as dirt. I'm thirsty and hot and it's been nearly twelve hours since I had a glass of water."

Silence hung heavy in the air between them as Scott

remembered the problem with the plumbing at his house, how there wasn't any water in the fridge. The air was suddenly a lot more arid than it should be.

Jack nodded toward the television. "Turn it off. Tell everyone to go home."

"What?"

"I'm serious. Forget grants and work, tell everybody to stock up on water and send them home."

The television faded to black, with a thin white line eventually shrinking to a dot in the middle which in turn became nothingness. "Where's the water going, Jack?"

CHAPTER 11

When the front door swung open and Scott ran in, Cam knew the shit was hitting the fan. Scott was a workaholic and didn't come home unless something was FUBAR. Even when he wasn't working he was working, tinkering with some experiment or gadget. Hell, even when he was just sitting he was learning, watching the Discovery Channel, reading some new science journal or something. Now, he looked spooked.

"Cam, get up and help me," he said, throwing his laptop and backpack of work gear on the chair near the door.

Before he knew what was going on, Cam was following Scott out to the garage, watching as the scientist threw boxes aside to get to the back of the room.

Becky followed them, holding Cobalt on her arms; the baby was crying again, further testament to the whole shit/fan scenario unfolding around them. "Scott, something's wrong with the water," she said.

"I know," Scott replied. "It's happening everywhere. Cam, help me get this thing down from the shelf."

From the top of a rickety wooden shelving unit, Cam grabbed one side of an old dehumidifier and got it safely to the ground. "This can make water, right?"

"It doesn't make it," Scott said, "but it'll pull it from the air, if there's any left to pull."

"Can we drink it?"

"Get the coffee filters from the cabinet in the kitchen. We can't drink it unless we can filter it."

After Scott had the dehumidifier plugged in, he took several large containers—metal thermoses, plastic pitchers, glass conifers, and something that looked like an astronaut's lunch pack—down from the shelf and carried them back into the house. "Becky, find me an empty milk carton. A cardboard one. Cam?"

Cam felt like a damn puppy as he trailed his brother-in-law into the living room. Scott was stuffing all the containers into his backpack, jamming them in as fast as he could. It was the kind of suitcase-stuffing people did knowing they were late for their flight. It didn't help that the baby was still crying. Suddenly, tensions were through the frigging roof.

"Cam?"

"What?"

"I need you to come with me to the reservoir. I need an extra set of hands."

"The reservoir? Why?"

Before Scott could answer him, Becky cut in, handing her brother the empty milk carton from the fridge. "Scott, this is scaring me. Why are you going to the reservoir?"

Tipping the carton upside down, Cam whacked it on the bottom. What looked like chunks of white dust fell to the floor. "Because we need to find water and we need to find it now."

Cam saw that Becky was near tears. She was a strong girl, and if she was losing it, it meant things were getting really fucked up. Instinct forced him to wrap his arms around her and tell her everything was going to be okay. She pulled away from him and gave him a glare that would turn a gorgon into stone. "Don't touch me. Don't you act like you love me after what you did."

"Beck, please, this is no time to—"

"What, Cam? No time to remind you that you fucked some girl behind my back when you had a kid and wife at home waiting for you. I don't care how much water disappears, that's one thing that *won't* ever disappear."

"Guys, you can fight later," Scott interjected, "I need Cam right now. While we're gone, Beck, lock the doors."

CHAPTER 12

The reservoir was about thirty minutes east of the house, nestled in the middle of rocky hills along the river. The access road leading to it was blocked off by a guardhouse, a new addition the city had installed as part of its anti-terrorism campaign. Scott was pretty sure terrorism had nothing to do with what was going on. Terrorists would lace the drinking supply with poison, not dry it up. When they got there and found the guardhouse empty, it didn't make much difference. Problem was, the large orange blockade arm was still down, stopping them from advancing.

"You gonna ram it?" Cam asked.

"I've got a better idea, Rambo." No use ruining the car when simple deductive reasoning would save the day, Scott thought as he got out of the car and opened the door to the guardhouse. Somehow he knew it was going to be unlocked—it was that kind of day. He pressed the green button on the console and the blockade arm rose up.

Once past the gate, they drove by the treatment facility and took a dirt access road that wound around to the far side of the reservoir. It was meant for all-terrain vehicles, like Jeeps and pickup trucks. Scott had been here once before for a work project, and he knew the dirt road was mostly used to monitor the fence that ran the perimeter of the reservoir. Again, part of the city's attempt to placate the citizens who believed Osama Bin Laden was skulking around the bushes of suburban San Diego County.

The reservoir had never been tampered with, and Scott was pretty sure the terrorists wouldn't bother with such a low-key act. Truth be told, it provided some of the best trout fishing in San Diego; if there was anything to worry about, it was getting a bad case of the Trout Trots.

There should have been some officials on patrol, but the road was unoccupied.

"I thought they had some guards here now. They on break?" Cam asked.

"I don't know. Why was there no guard at the front?"

Cam spotted something and said, "Look, there's a bunch of cars over there."

Three quarters of the way around the reservoir, toward the rear of the sterilization facility, a group of cars was parked on the side of the road. Scott slowed the car and squinted across the large body of water, trying to make out what was going on. There was a lot of activity, nearly forty people trying to get into the water. City police and the guards were fighting them off. Many of them had containers much like the ones Scott had brought.

"What do you make of that?" Cam asked.

"My guess, they suspect terrorist activity and figure someone's tampering with the water."

"Those yahoos don't look like terrorists to me."

"They aren't. They're just thirsty."

"What if they come arrest us?"

Scott shook his head, trying to make sense of the situation. "Can't arrest us for drinking out of the reservoir. Might arrest us for tampering with the drinking supply if they suspect we're part of something bigger."

"Check out that pig," Cam said. "That cop just threw a punch."

"People are starting to panic, not think. If half the world had an education none of this would be getting out of hand."

"Speak for yourself, Brainboy, school sucked."

"I'll pretend you didn't say that. Okay, quick, grab a couple containers and when I say go we're going to race down to the water and fill up each one. Make sure you fill each one."

"What does it matter?" asked Cam, taking the thermos and glass conifer from the backpack.

"I need to determine if the substance holding the water makes a difference somehow."

"Seems like it don't. I was at the store today."

"Seems that way, but we can't be sure till we rule it out."

"I'm pretty sure—"

"Cam, I went to bat for you last night with my sister, now shut up and quit giving me lip."

"Yes, sir, Mr. Fitch, sir."

"I'm serious here, Cam."

Bang!

He and Cam both jumped at the gunshot.

"Holy shit," Cam said, pointing across the water,

"that cop just shot somebody!"

The crowd had turned away from the reservoir and was now fighting the police. Fists were flying, legs kicking, and they fell to the ground in a heap. Another shot rang out and another body rolled into the water.

"Jesus Christ, this is not good," Scott said, opening the car door. "This is getting out of control real fucking fast."

"I don't know about this, Scott. Let's just get out—"

"Do you know you have a kid at home who can only go two, maybe three days without water? Look at me! Do you know that?!"

Yelling was never something Scott did if he could avoid it, but Cam's eyes were showing fear and hesitation. It was a moment of shock. Scott was feeling it too, but he knew it could be fought. Cam was a tough motherfucker, six feet tall, lots of muscles from all his days surfing. If he gave in to fear they were truly in a heap of shit.

"Cam?! Are you hearing me?"

With true surfer-be-damned attitude, Cam nodded and said, "Yeah, got it. No fear, right? Gotta get Cobe water."

"Okay, be fast. Go!"

Keeping his eyes on the melee across the way, Scott ran down to the water and dunked each container in as quickly as he could. A fast look around at the rock walls of the reservoir showed the watermark was about five feet higher than the water. It didn't take a scientist to know what that meant. The reservoir was disappearing. Its size was the only reason it was doing it at a slower rate than anything in a regular carton or glass.

He filed that knowledge away. Maybe they could get to a lake or something if the situation got worse.

"Um, Scott?"

Scott looked up and immediately saw what concerned Cam. Across the reservoir, the mob had dissipated. Two men lay on the ground, and one more floated in the water. The police, eight of them, were slapping handcuffs on the ones too slow to get away. The problem was that they had spotted him and Cam.

"You full up?"

"I am now," Cam replied.

"Get in the car. Now."

It was wishful thinking to believe they were going to get out of this easily. The police were getting in their cars. With lights flashing, they headed around the reservoir in the opposite direction of Cam and Scott, racing to cut through the facility's staff parking lot and meet them at the guardhouse.

"What now?" Cam asked.

"I don't know. I don't want to get shot."

"Dump the water?"

"Then we may be just as dead."

Neither said a word as Scott drove the car back toward the guardhouse, his fingers pressed tight like white slugs against the steering wheel. The police cruisers were nearing the parking lot on the other side of the fence, about to appear at any moment. Scott's heart raced and threatened to rip out of his chest. Maybe they should just dump the water, play dumb and hope for the best, he thought.

The cops didn't appear.

"Where are they?" Cam asked, trying to keep the water from spilling out of the containers he had wedged between his legs.

Good question, Scott thought. Had they taken another road beyond the guardhouse? Were they waiting for them on the main road? Cars parked across the road in true police roadblock fashion, guns drawn and ready to fire through the windshield?

As he neared the guardhouse, he found out it was none of the above. A chain-link fence surrounded the staff parking lot. Probably a new addition, Scott thought, an attempt to keep trespassers out. A large chain and lock was wrapped around its gate. The police couldn't get through, and the only way to reach the guardhouse now would be to double back all the way around. Or not: one of the officers was running to the fence, shoving his gun through the hole in the wire. Was he going to shoot them? What the hell was getting into people?

"Hang on!" Scott yelled. Luck had thrown them a bone and he wasn't about to waste it no matter how well maintained his car was.

The car plowed though the blockade arm and tore it off, exploding it into splinters that fired straight into the sky. The car jerked as the hood dented inwards. Both Scott and Cam were thrown around in their seats, some of the water spilling into their laps.

"You okay?" Scott asked as they sped onto the main road.

"Yeah," Cam replied, "fine." But his eyes were

closed and his jaw clenched. He stayed that way for the next couple of minutes, until Scott told him no one was following.

CHAPTER 13

Rebecca was watching the dehumidifier, but wasn't really seeing it. Her mind was on a single track, fearful that Scott and Cam were in some sort of trouble. The television played low in the background, the news about the ocean was on every channel. Channel 10 interviewed a man about the water in his pool, Channel 6 was showing pictures of dead fish on the ground, and Fox had a reporter in London standing beside the Thames, which was slowly getting lower.

When she was able to get her mind off Scott and Cam, it flitted to Cobalt. His crying, his discomfort, his apparent thirst was sounding every alarm in her head. This was her son, her life, for whom she'd gladly die a thousand times to save from harm. But how the hell was she supposed to make water? If Cobe hadn't been born prematurely and put on oxygen for two weeks, she'd just breastfeed him. But he'd missed those important first days of learning how to suckle, and she'd never been able to produce milk as a result. Cobe depended on formula and it was evaporating. How was she supposed to keep him healthy? Why would God do this to her child?

The pan in the dehumidifier was bone dry, which was doing nothing for her fears. Cobe was lying on a baby blanket in the living room, his crying having abated for a moment. A rattle jingled every couple of seconds, his favorite one, the one Cam had bought when they were living the proverbial American Dream.

What was she going to do with Cam? God, she was so pissed at him, so hurt by what he'd done. Could she really forgive him for something so painful? "No way," she spoke to the empty room. Still, she did love him, and needed to know he was safe. Why couldn't he have just come home that night, gotten in bed with her, had sex with her? Wasn't she still attractive to him? Funny how when he was around all she could think about was punching him, but when he was gone, she missed him terribly.

It wasn't fair.

The rattle shook in the other room. Cobe was still occupied with his toy. That was good, that gave her a minute to think.

She stepped out onto the front porch and looked down the road for her brother and husband, but saw no one. The closest neighbors, the Moores, were a good hundred yards away. Although they were old and quiet and she rarely spoke to them, she was confident she could go there if she needed help.

But, then, what could they do? What she needed was water, juice, milk, anything to drink. God, her thirst had come on strong in the last couple hours. The jug of water Cam had brought was nearly gone. At first she thought it better to ration it, but it was going to disappear if she didn't drink it, so she'd filled Cobe's bottle and had a glass herself. There was enough left for a half a glass each once Cam and Scott got back.

As she looked around the yard, she noticed the grass was dead. That wasn't something she'd normally notice; most summers were pretty dry in Southern California. Today, it really stuck out. Maybe it was because so many of the trees looked dry as well. The succulents Scott had planted were faring no better; half of them were turning brown.

"Come on, just rain or something," she said, staring at the sky. "Please, God, I don't understand any of this."

When she looked back down she spotted Scott's car coming up the road, kicking up dust in its wake.

"Thank fucking Christ."

CHAPTER 14

Cam leapt out of the car before it was even parked, ran to Becky and threw his arms around her. He didn't care if she shoved him away, he needed her in his arms. He needed to know how she felt. What if something like the reservoir happened again, but ended differently?

"Cam, you're squeezing . . . I can't breathe."

He released her and looked deep in her eyes, deep into their past. He saw the times they'd spent long weekends at the beach, laughing, surfing and having sex in the back of his car. "I'm sorry. I'm sorry about what I did. I don't want to lose you."

She was on the verge of tears when she spoke. "You already did, Cam. You already did."

Her words floored him. How could she not forgive him, especially now, when things were getting so fucking strange and scary?

"But, Beck—"

"No, Cam. No."

The pain began in his gut, set his stomach bubbling. There is no moment so potent, he thought as his insides twisted, as the moment you lose the love you took for granted. The feel of the other girl in his arms was still fresh, and he hated it. He wanted to erase it and replace it with the feel of Becky in his arms. What had he done?

"The plants are all dying," Scott said, stopping near the door of the house for a moment. In his hands he carried the containers full of water, the water that had almost cost them their lives. "Cam, get the rest from the car."

Becky followed her brother inside and Cam stole the moment to be alone with his self-pity. Perhaps it would be better if he just left. Clearly she didn't want him around, despite what Scott had told him. No, he had to stay, there was Cobe to think about. Whether Becky knew it or not, they were all going to need each other if things got worse.

When she poked her head out the door a few seconds later he almost expected her to shoo him away, but instead she waved him in and said, "Come on, I saved you some water."

He grabbed the rest of the containers from the car and rushed inside, his hangdog expression picking up a little. Scott was placing the reservoir water in the fridge and Cam followed suit. Empty juice bottles still filled the top shelf of the fridge, and the food was drying up. There was one of those store-bought rotisserie chickens in there that looked like a mound of sun-baked yellow PlayDoh. Scott poured some water into a Tupperware cup and placed it in the freezer, obviously thinking that ice would last longer. The only problem with that theory was that the freezer was nearly devoid of the ice that had already been in there; it was disappearing as quickly as the liquids.

"It's skipping phase." Scott rubbed his finger around the walls of the freezer. "No moisture. How the hell can it . . . " He trailed off and went into the garage, leaving Cam and Becky in the kitchen together.

"We have to give some to Cobe," Cam said.

Becky's eyes were puffy and she looked on the edge of crying.

Would they be able to cry? Would their tears dry up, he wondered. What was going to happen to them? What happens to the body when it runs out of water? He'd seen the commercial on TV where starving children in Africa sat half naked on the ground, their bellies distended like a tire pumped too full of air. Flies buzzing around them like tiny vultures waiting for a newly-dead meal. He couldn't let that happen to his son. He just couldn't.

"He's got some in his bottle now," Becky said. Then, opening the fridge, she took the jug of water out and poured him a glass. "Here, drink."

"What about you?"

"I already had some. And Scott drank from it before you came in."

"Shouldn't we try and—"

"No," said Scott, returning from the garage. "We should hydrate ourselves now. Get any amount of water into us before it goes away. If we don't, and we wait, we're wasting it. I'll keep a little in each container to see what happens."

"You think one of those containers will be able to hold it?"

"I don't know. All I know is the scientific method and that says we keep testing until we can officially rule stuff out. I'll tell you this much, my hopes aren't high."

"Then why freeze it?" Cam asked.

"Same reasoning. At least, I thought it was worth a shot until I looked in the freezer. Obviously any form of water is just vanishing. I don't get it. There's no physical explanation for it. Matter doesn't just skip through phases when changing. Science doesn't support it."

From the living room, Cobe began cooing.

"I'll refill his bottle," Cam said.

No one said anything to him. No one seemed to even know what to say.

Together, they all went into the living room and stared down at the blue-eyed baby on the floor. His tiny feet were kicking the air with amusement, his head swiveling to take them all in. As if to mock the whole situation, his chubby little face broke into a smile.

The empty baby bottle lay on the blanket.

DAY THREE

CHAPTER 15

The night passed slowly. Slow like an old man backtracking through a speech because he's forgetting important parts. Slow like an emergency room doctor who says he'll be with you in a minute. Slow like flies waiting for a starving baby to roll its eyes back in its head and exhale its last fragile breath.

There was no way for Scott to get his mind off what was happening. Before he'd gone to bed he'd called Jack, but there was no answer and, thus far, he'd gotten no call back. He'd also stood by as Cam called his parents up in the Bay area and got no reply.

The sum of those two things was concerning, but really equaled squat at the end of the day. Could be people were just panicked and out looking for water. Could be those towns used hydroelectricity and were out of power. Could be anything, really, so it wouldn't do to freak out about it until they knew the truth.

By six in the morning Scott had managed to drift in and out of sleep enough that he'd gotten maybe two and a half hours of recharge power. Not really enough to go on, but enough to last for a little while. Throwing off the sheet, he looked at the empty glass on his night stand. There'd been a quarter cup of water in it last night.

He made his way to the bathroom and peed, but what came out was about a tablespoon's worth of urine. The water in his body was running low, a bad sign of things to come. In fact, he could feel a dull cramp in his abdomen already, which was most likely his body trying to draw even the smallest amount of water from the waste in his guts, constipating him.

In the kitchen, he opened the fridge and took out each container. All of them were empty. The Tupperware container in the freezer was bone dry as well.

He dropped it in the sink and let it bounce around in the dry basin, the urge to scream lingering at the base of his throat. Through the window above the sink, he looked out at the front yard and saw the succulents were red and brown, the trees were without leaves, the grass was yellow and sharp.

It's all going away, he thought, every last bit of it. Anything that relies on water.

Why?

Even knowing there had to be a scientific answer, he found himself turning to the small crucifix hanging over the entrance to the living room. The now familiar sense of duality he'd been dealing with since the accident rose in him once again. The crucifix belonged to his mother . . . had belonged to her, anyway, before the powers that be saw fit to take her from this world.

"There's a reason for this," he said, defying it. He knew being insolent with a piece of wood was stupid, but he needed to say this. "Someone's gonna figure it out. Scientifically. Because I refuse to believe, even if you do exist, that you'd do it this way. It's cruel. It's going to hurt."

The crucifix remained still, a piece of wall art without a voice. Its silent decree blanketed the world, foretelling the end of days.

All over the globe, thought Scott. The news last night had mostly talked about San Diego, but touched on the phenomena in other countries. Perhaps there'd been a breakthrough overnight.

He turned on the television in the living room, flipped to CNN, and froze solid at the image on the screen.

A reporter stood on an observation deck in front of a sheer rock cliff. A sign next to the man read Niagara Falls. Scott turned the volume up and caught the last bit of the man's report. " . . . only God knows why this once majestic waterfall no longer runs. Back to you."

Scott flipped to one of the local stations. Instead of the morning talk show that usually ran, the station was flashing images of lakes that had run dry. People milled about in front of them, looking confused and scared. The image flashed to a riot in Sacramento, where people stormed a water bottling company and cops fought them off with rubber bullets.

"Lucky you're not here," Scott said, talking to the people on TV, remembering the killing at the reservoir yesterday. "At least your bullets are only rubber."

"What's the word," Cam said, walking up in his underwear. "Tell me we have water. I'm fucking thirsty."

"We have nothing, Cam. Nothing."

Cam finally noticed the images on the television and

went silent. Together, they watched video footage come in from across the globe, sitting down when they saw the pictures of people dying in third world countries.

"They were already starving, their water scarce," Scott said. "Now they're in the process of dying."

"Look," Cam said. "Is that the ocean?"

The television showed the continental shelf exposed to the open air. All manner of crustaceans and fish lay unmoving on the ground. When the camera panned, the dead sea life formed a slick, silvery blanket on the newly-exposed land. About a half mile out from the shelf, the water lapped lightly against the ground. On this new shore, fish, still a bit wet, flopped about desperately searching for the tide, popping into the air like spring toys where seagulls swooped down and caught them in their bills. "Yeah," Scott replied. "It's still here but it's lost of lot of water. It'll be gone in a day or two at this rate."

"So will we."

"Must be the salt keeping it from disappearing as fast as the fresh water."

"How's that?"

"Wish I knew. Water is water. Like the food in the fridge, it can evaporate out of a substance, leaving the remaining ingredients behind. My guess is that dry ocean floor is covered in salt."

"Doesn't tell me why it's taking longer for the ocean," Cam replied.

"Nope. But it doesn't matter either. You can't drink seawater."

From the bedroom, Cobe started crying. Cam and

Scott looked at each other. Their glance spoke of the need to find the baby some water.

Becky appeared a moment later with Cobe in her arms. "Please, give him some water."

Scott just shook his head; he couldn't say the words.

Maybe that was worse than not hearing it outright, because Becky began trembling, shaking her head back and forth, "No. No no no no! He needs to drink. He needs water or juice or something!" With the baby in her arms she went to the fridge and took out a jar of baby food. When she opened it and looked inside she swore and slammed it on the counter.

Scott had never seen his sister like this, not even when Cam had cheated on her and broken her heart. Not that she didn't let her emotions out when she had to, but now she was on the verge of hysteria. She was losing it, and he couldn't really blame her, could he? He went over and looked in the baby food jar, saw the hard, dry food. All the moisture had gone out of it. It looked like dried paint.

"What are we going to do?" Becky asked.

Cam ran to her and hugged her and the baby. But despite her breakdown she was still holding her grudge and shrugged him off. Instead of testing her anger, he gently led them to the couch and told her they'd figure something out. Scott was glad that little scene hadn't erupted, considering Becky's mental state.

Eventually, they sat and watched the television, and Cobe fell asleep.

Time passed, like water from the earth.

For the next several hours, the news confirmed

what everyone already knew. The earth's water was simply disappearing; in fact, much of it was already gone. The ice caps were receding by the minute. The oceans were faring better, but were still shrinking into nonexistence.

People were dying.

Scott didn't know the exact facts of how long a person could live without water, but he knew it was pretty damn short. A few days at most. Beyond a week and you were denying your cells the fuel they needed to live. Beyond a week and you were a goner.

"You cannot destroy matter," Scott finally said. "You can't just get rid of it."

"What's that mean?" Cam asked.

"It means . . . the water has to go somewhere."

"Where?"

"Usually . . . into the air."

"Oh, yeah, I remember that from school."

"Considering the amount that should already be in the air, it should be a deluge outside."

"It's not."

"I know."

Becky looked up from where her son lay on the couch next to her. Apparently, there was still enough moisture in her body to make tears. "Scott . . . please?"

What? What did she expect him to do? He was doing his best to work this out but he was just a geologist. The planet had thousands of brilliant scientists far more qualified to solve this than he. How come they weren't on television telling everyone to remain calm? Did they know something the rest of the world didn't?

Jack. He had to speak to Jack.

The cell phone was still on his nightstand. He rushed to his room, snatched it up and dialed his boss. This time, Jack answered.

"Jack, where have you—"

"Scott, I'm at the La Posta aquifer! They're going crazy—"

The line went dead, but not before Scott heard someone screaming.

Adrenaline flushed Scott's system and he dialed 911, pressing the buttons so fast he botched the call and had to redial. The phone rang and rang but no one answered. Finally a message came on saying that an operator would be with him as soon as possible. "Shit. Everyone's calling."

He ran into the living room, grabbed his car keys off the table. "Jack's in trouble."

"Who the fuck is Jack?" Cam asked.

"My boss. I called him and he was screaming and . . . he was at the La Posta site. I think there may be water there."

As if jolted by electricity Becky stood up and grabbed Scott's shoulders. "Are you sure?"

"No. Not at all. But it sounded like he was in a fight. It's possible that . . . see, the La Posta site is miles deep. The water seeps through the continental shelf and floods this large underground cavern."

"And the ocean is still here at a certain level," Cam said, following the logic. "But wait, you can't drink ocean water."

"Not straight you can't. But there are machines at

the University that'll purify it."

"So if we can get some—"

"Which is what I think Jack was trying to do."

"Won't it disappear quicker if you make it regular water?" Cam asked.

"Don't know. I bet Jack was testing that theory. Or was about to, anyway."

"How do people know about the site?" Becky asked.

"We work with the city. Lots of people know about it. Could be it's our own workers, could be those workers told people. I don't know. But I'm going to find out."

"I'm coming," Cam said.

Scott waited to see if Becky was going to protest, but she remained silent. He could see she wanted to say something, wanted to tell Cam to stay. She was still hurting from Cam's infidelity, and she wasn't going to let him off the hook that easily. For now she was letting pride control her. Damn, she was stubborn, just like their mother had been.

"Okay, get your shoes and let's go."

CHAPTER 16

Cam didn't know rocks but he sure as shit knew cars, and right now the engine in Scott's SUV was pinging and ponging like someone had left a handful of ball bearings under the hood.

"You've got no water in your radiator. You're going to overheat and warp the head. You're probably out of oil as well."

"I'll take the chance," Scott said, pressing the accelerator to the floor, backing out of the driveway.

"Stop! Seriously, the car won't get further than a mile or two tops."

"Mineral oil might work. They use it in some computers."

"Mineral oil? Did Becky go through all that baby oil we had? We bought a box of it at Costco."

"No. I don't even think she uses it. It's in the bathroom in the linen closet. You know it has mineral oil in it?"

"Yeah. Used to read the bottle when I took a shit." Without hesitation, Cam rushed inside and returned a moment later with a handful of BeeBee's Baby Oil bottles. He held them up to let Scott see that they still contained liquid..

"Thank God you're cheap," Scott said, knowing that the expensive brands these days substituted the mineral oil for water and plant extract.

As soon as Scott popped the hood Cam unscrewed the cap for the radiator and emptied a couple of bottles into it. When he was done, he put the remaining full bottle in the car and climbed in. Scott turned the ignition and let the thermostat heat up, waiting to see if the car would stall. The needle rose toward the red but stopped just beneath it. "Hang on," Scott said, "not sure how long this is gonna last."

They drove with the radio on, neither of them talking. Every station was addressing the water problem and the consensus was not good; none of the authorities had any fucking clue what was going on. FEMA, DOE, DOA, even radical groups like Greenpeace were dumbfounded, though they certainly were making their theories known about it being retribution for raping the land.

"Water has to go somewhere," Scott said. "It has to."

"Huh?"

"The water. After we find Jack I think we should swing by the university and track the weather patterns over the Pacific."

"Don't you think the weather people are doing that?"

Scott shook his head, the kind of shake that said Cam wasn't following him. "Weather over the Pacific is hard to predict. They don't have the satellite setup here they do on the east coast. They can't really predict the storms until they see them. All I'm saying is, the water can't just be going nowhere. If we can find some storm fronts—"

"And if not? Look, there aren't even any clouds in the sky."

"I've noticed."

Again they shut up and listened to the radio, Cam studying the blue sky for any trace of clouds, anything that might constitute a storm. Finally, Cam turned it off and said, "I don't feel good. I mean, I'm really frigging thirsty, Scott. It kind of . . . it kind of hurts."

"I know. My gut is tight and my head is beginning to pound. It's dehydration, like being drunk."

"Being drunk ain't so bad. I've gone days being drunk."

"It's not supposed to be a badge of honor, you know."

"I'm just saying, I can deal with drunk."

"This will be more like when you have the flu."

"Oh, that's bad. Will it hurt to die like this?"

"We're not gonna die."

"But if there's no water . . . " Cam didn't finish the thought. He was sure he was right in this—they were going to die—but maybe this wasn't the best time to dwell on it—not when they were on a rescue mission. When the ache in his stomach grew so bad he couldn't ignore it any longer, then he'd bring it up again.

An abandoned car sat in the middle of the road like some giant sleeping metal animal. Scott cut around it and watched it recede in the driver's side mirror. "Must have broken down," he said.

Sure, thought Cam, everybody leaves their cars in the middle of the road when they break down. A quarter-mile later he saw an elderly man lying on the side of the road, his appendages splayed out and bent like spider legs. The man's face was sunken, the crotch of his pants stained brown. One of his shoes was further back in the middle of the road, like the guy had walked to his grave.

"What the fuck," Cam said, "is he dead?"

Scott pulled the SUV over to the side of the road and got out, leaving the motor running. He approached the body carefully, felt for a pulse before confirming to Cam the man was dead.

"He shit himself?" Cam asked as Scott climbed back in the truck.

"Yeah, your bowels release when you die. He was old, maybe already ill, had no fluids to get better." Scott took out his cell phone and dialed 911, but again there was no answer. After a minute he put the phone away and strapped on his seatbelt. "We gotta get to Jack."

For the next ten minutes they drove well above the speed limit, racing to get to the La Posta site. There were a few cars out driving around (no doubt running on a variety of different coolants), including police cars, but Cam was willing to bet nobody was getting a ticket today for speeding. Once all the cars stalled, how much longer would the police even patrol? Officers needed water too, and unless they had a secret stash of it, they'd soon be getting sick like everyone else.

What then? Chaos? Every man for himself? How was he supposed to help Becky and Cobalt when that type of shit hit the fan?

"Check that out." He pointed through the windshield.

Scott followed the trajectory of Cam's finger to a supermarket where hordes of people were throwing bottles and rocks into the store through the front window. Many of them looked sick, their faces starting to wrinkle. One of them put a hand to her head and fell over.

"Shit, did you see that?" Cam yelled.

"They're looking for water. They're blaming the store for not having any. It's starting."

"What's starting?"

"Mob mentality. Anger displacement. Panic. It's gonna get bad."

Through the broken window a group of men pulled the manager out of the store, shoved him to the parking lot pavement and circled around him. The man sat on his knees, blood running down his head, pleading to be left alone. Someone picked up a shopping cart and brought it down on his head with the force of a crosstown train. The man's skull split wide, spit something gray onto the pavement, and he fell to the ground as the people kicked him.

"Jesus Christ!" Cam yelled.

"Yeah, let's get outta here."

Down the road they saw another group of people hovering around a fire hydrant, beating it with lead pipes. A mile or so past that they came upon a family of four—mother, father, two little boys—pulling a manhole cover up and starting down it. More cars began to line the roads, their engines assuredly overheated. No steam came from any of them, which Cam found weird. They were just dead. A number of people were on the street with signs begging for water. Nobody had a sign offering it.

The last idle car they passed had a woman in it who appeared to be sleeping, but Cam knew different. Her eyes and mouth were open, a rictus gasping for anything wet.

His thoughts immediately flicked to Cobalt. If older people were already dying of dehydration, how long would it be before his son fell victim to it? What would he do if he had to hold his dead son's body in his arms? How did he go on living if that happened? And what of Becky? Was he supposed to die alone, without her?

"Gimme that." Scott pointed to the security club he kept on the passenger side floor.

Cam picked it up and handed it over. There was no need to ask what Scott's intentions were; he could see the site drawing close, could see the horde of people that were crowded around the management trailer. Their faces were flushed and their lips cracked. A disheveled man came out the trailer and shook his head. At this the crowd ambled over to a pipe sticking up out of the ground and started fiddling with some dials on a nearby control box.

"That's Dick Lawson," Scott said, pointing to the disheveled man, who was now messing with the box as well. "He works for the city. Shit, he must think there's drinking water in the damn aquifer. Idiot doesn't know it's salt. Stay close to me. I have a feeling Jack is in the trailer."

"Whoa whoa whoa."
"What?"

"What do you mean 'what?' You're holding a fucking headcrusher and I got nothing."

"I'm not looking for violence."

"And I wasn't looking to be a dad but shit happens."

"So get a weapon."

"Where? You want me to throw this Alanis Morissette CD at them? Alanis Morissette, man! Tell me you got this free from Columbia House or something."

Scott grabbed the CD and threw it in the backseat. "Leave the damn CDs alone. There's an emergency roadside kit in back. I think it's got a mini crowbar thing in it. Grab that."

Cam climbed into the back, wondering why his brother-in-law had such shitty taste in music. Not that this was the time to discuss it, he thought, but it was better than focusing on the impending violence the need for a weapon implied. He found the crowbar in question. It was just as Scott had described, a smaller version of an actual crowbar, definitely enough to do some damage. He hefted it in his hand and gave it a swing, almost shattering the back window.

"Try not to bust the truck, I'm still paying for it," Scott said.

"Alanis Morissette," Cam replied, as if that answered everything.

The front door opened and Scott got out. Cam opened the rear door and met him around the front.

The first thing he noticed was how hot the air was. They were near the ocean but there wasn't any of the usual breeze coming off it. The smell of salt and brine, usually strong and thick, was nonexistent. Not to mention everyone was kicking up dirt and sand, making the air as abrasive as sandpaper.

Cam's thirst went up a notch. His belly rumbled and spit, and he felt a dull ache begin near his intestines. Parts of him felt itchy with dryness. He needed a drink soon. Real soon. Even the ocean water Scott said was under the ground didn't seem like such a bad idea right now. At least it would be water.

God, he was so damned thirsty.

"What's going on, Dick?" Scott shouted.

Cam noticed his brother-in-law's lips were beginning to split. He was sweating, and the pigment was draining from his face, which meant he was losing whatever fluids he still had left.

The man messing with the control box looked up. "Mr. Fitch?"

"Scott."

"Yeah, Scott. I remember you."

"Where's Jack?"

Dick suddenly looked like a man under the beam of a police flashlight. Bad deeds were written into the creases around his dry, red eyes.

"Where's Jack?" Scott repeated. "In the trailer. He had water, Scott. We just wanted to share it. That's all. Don't think we planned for it to happen—"

Cam barely had time to notice Scott wasn't standing beside him anymore; his brother-in-law took off like a bullet, leaving him to stare down twelve or thirteen men (and one woman) by himself. Each one looked desperate. Real fucking scared. Like civilized thought had suddenly become an archaic idea. The need for water was cutting rationality into slices of primal instinct, and Cam was keenly aware that he was outnumbered.

Slowly, he waved to Dick, friendly-like, and made his way into the trailer. He even smiled like a dumb asshole to show he was no threat.

Inside, he found Scott leaning over a man's body, feeling its neck for a pulse. The man's head had a huge gash in it, and blood was pooled underneath it. At least our blood hasn't dried up, Cam thought. "That Jack?" he asked.

"Was, anyway."

"They killed him? Oh shit, tell me they didn't kill him."

"They didn't kill him."

"Seriously?"

"Wake up, Cam. Yes, they killed him."

"Good old Fitch sarcasm. Thought that was Becky's trait?"

"Runs in the family. Look out."

Snatching the security club off the table where he'd laid it, Scott rushed back outside. Through the window Cam watched as he ran up to Dick and got in the man's personal space. Heated words filled the air between them. Dick was saying something about Jack having drinking water, but when Cam looked around, he didn't see anything with water in it. Nothing was even wet.

"He had a cup of water," Dick yelled. "We're fucking dying of thirst and you fucking scientists have got water, so don't act like—"

"Nobody has water," Scott answered, the club in front of him like a sword. "You murdered him."

"You don't even look thirsty. How is that? Do you have water, too?"

"Why? Are you going to kill me?"

The crowd started circling around Scott, some of them carrying tools, others with fists balled. They think he has water, Cam realized. They're going to rush him and then what? Then I'll be left alone with these crazies. They probably assume I'm a scientist too. I have to get Scott out of here.

"Scott," Cam yelled, stepping back out into the open air, making mental notes of who was carrying what and how quickly he could make it to the SUV. He might even get away, if the keys were in the ignition. Of course they wouldn't be, because this wasn't a movie.

So, really, he was fucked.

"Cam, get Jack's body and put it in the truck," Scott said without looking back. Then to Dick: "He has a wife."

"And he'd be seeing her if he'd just shared his water," Dick said. "He wouldn't give us any. That's murder in my eyes. So maybe we're even Steven now." Dick pointed to the control box, said, "Tell us how to operate this thing so we can get some too. We know it's down there. You're keeping it from us."

For the first time, Cam noticed that some of the people were opening a valve on the tube sticking up from the ground. The aquifer was under there, and in it vast quantities of sea water, or so Scott said.

"You drink the water that's down there and you'll die, too."

The crowd roared. Someone shouted, "Make him get it," another yelled, "Break his fingers until he tells."

Jesus, Scott, Cam thought, just fucking tell them.

He didn't have to. All Dick's button pressing and knob turning caused a small geyser to shoot from the pipe. The people rushed at it, shoving and pushing as they threw their mouths over it. A couple of them coughed and gagged, the sea water caustic in their system, but they kept gulping. It looked so refreshing even Cam was tempted.

"No need," Dick said, smiling. "Now we've got your water."

"You're an idiot, Dick. You and your friends are going to die sooner if you drink that. Be my guest."

As Scott made his way back to the trailer all Cam could think was, thank God. It's not that he couldn't hold his own in a fight—there'd been a few rough nights at the bar when he'd assisted the bouncers with rowdy drunks—but two against thirteen was a losing battle.

"Come on," Scott said, climbing back in the trailer. "Help me get his body."

"Shouldn't we call the cops?"

"Cops don't care about this. No one's answering 911. When we get home we barricade the house and load Dad's gun. Can you shoot?"

"Hell yeah."

"I mean really shoot, not just think you can because you played Nintendo or something."

"Yeah, I've shot guns. I'll manage."

"Good. We need a tarp or something, check that

storage closet over there. The combo for the lock is 11-9-64, Jack's birthday."

Cam stepped over the body and undid the lock on the storage closet. The front door was bent inward and marred like someone had been trying to break into it. No doubt the crazies outside thought Jack had hidden something in it.

When he flung wide the door he saw they were right.

Cam backpedaled over to where Scott was rolling the body up on its side. "Um, Scott . . ."

"Find a tarp?"

"Found something else."

The words were mysterious and weighty enough to cause Scott to spin around with the club in his hand. Slowly, he lowered it by his side as they both looked at the collection of jars on the shelves in the closet. Each had about a quarter cup of water in it. There were maybe twenty jars total.

"They were right," Cam said. "Jack had water."

As if afraid to touch them, Scott hesitantly took one out, popped off its lid, and drank the liquid inside. When he was done he licked his lips and sighed. "It's water. Drinkable. How the hell did he save all this? In glass jars? We tried glass."

"Maybe the closet protected it?"

"No. Nothing hermetic about this storage closet."

Cam didn't answer, just rushed to the nearest jar, tore its lid off and drank it down. "Oh fucking Christ that's good."

From outside came several yells as the people

around the observation well continued to gulp down the sea water. Cam gripped his weapon a little tighter, seeing that Scott was doing the same. If any of the people outside saw there was water in here, they were as good as dead.

"Here." Scott rushed over and made sure the door was locked. "Pour all the water into that jug there on the bottom shelf, and then put it in that box there. We'll say it's Jacks belongings. Leave one full jar for the idiots outside."

"Why leave anything? They're murderers."

"Because I'm not. But I'm not rewarding them for this either."

As quickly as he could, Cam tore the covers off the jars and filled the small plastic jug. When he was done, he had about a half gallon of water. He snapped the lid on top of it, held it closed and shook it to make sure it was sealed up tight. "We got to get this home to Cobe and Becky quick. I think it's already evaporating."

"It isn't evaporating. It's just disappearing," Scott said, checking out the window on the people at the pump. "If it was just evaporating we'd be pulling it from the air and there'd be ice . . . in the . . . freezer."

The way Scott's voice slowed concerned Cam. "What're you looking at?"

"The ground around the well should be a hell of a lot more wet than that. If I had time I could calculate the rate of loss—"

"I'll calculate it: fast. Real fucking fast. How's that?"

"Close enough. Okay, we're gonna have to hurry."

"Are we still taking Jack?"

Turning away from the window, Scott went over and tried to lift Jack's body up. Cam could tell the corpse was heavy, probably somewhere in the realm of 200 pounds. It would take a good many minutes to get him in the truck before they could leave. If the water was still disappearing as fast as it was, that was time they couldn't afford to lose.

Scott must have known this because he whispered something in Jack's ear, something sorrowful by the look of it, and then stood up. "We'll come for him later."

"What's that?" Cam pointed to a saucepan on the floor of the closet. The inside of the pan was coated with a white powder and bits of what looked like sand.

"Don't know," Scott said, picking it up and smelling it. He rubbed his hand over it, covering his fingers in white powder, and brought his fingers to his mouth. Tentatively, he licked them. "Shit. So that's how he did it. It's third grade science."

"Did what?"

Scott smiled. "This powder, it's—"

"You son of a bitch."

Cam spun around, found Dick peeking in through the window, his face covered in salt water and his eyes bulging and pink. He was staring at the water jug in Cam's arms, fixated on the liquid inside.

Before Cam had time to think, Dick was smashing the window with a rock and screaming, "Water! They have water!"

Everything went to hell real fucking fast.

The window in the door exploded as a lead pipe

crashed through it, glass shards flying inward at Cam and Scott like angry wasps. Sunburned arms thrust through the broken window like something out of a zombie movie and undid the lock. At the same time, Dick was almost all the way through the window, his eyes locked on the salvation in Cam's arms.

"Water! Water!" they all screamed. It might as well have been "Kill them! Kill them!" as far as Cam was concerned.

He grabbed his mini crowbar and raised it above his head, his stomach erupting in a ball of tightness, ready to strike Dick down. Ready to kill? He hoped not. But something instinctual rose up inside him and he knew that if it came down to himself or these bastards, it was going to be himself. They sure as hell didn't look like they wanted to talk.

"Cam!" Scott yelled as the door flung wide.

Like a single creature with multiple arms, legs, and heads, the crowd rushed in and threw Scott to the floor, everyone swinging their tools and sticks at him. They smothered him like a giant blanket, began pounding him with anything hard. Somewhere under the pile, Scott grunted and reeled in pain as each blow hit home.

Cam was on them in a heartbeat, swinging his crowbar at the blonde woman who sat on top of the pile. Her head split wide and she toppled to the floor. No time to think about what he was doing, though. He aimed for a large man in a Padres shirt next, but was slammed sideways as Dick's fist, like a battering ram, connected with the side of his head.

The jug fell from his arms and slid under the

nearby desk.

"Get the water!" Dick yelled.

The crowd must have thought Scott still had it, because none of them rushed to the desk; they kept wailing on their prey.

"Cam!" came Scott's muffled cry. His arm found its way out from under the pile of people. It was drenched in blood, the fingers purple from being stepped on. His next scream was cut short with a gurgle.

Wooziness passed like a wave through Cam as he tried to right himself. A fog overtook him and he slumped to the ground again. Concussion, he thought. Not good. They'd kill him if he didn't get up.

Dick was clawing under the desk for the water, like a rat tearing into a trash bag. No, thought Cam, that water was for Cobe and Becky, not these murderers. His baby was going to die without it.

Dick had the water jug now and was yanking the top off of it. Cam wanted to rush the man, to swing that crowbar into his eyes, but his head hurt too much to fight. Where was the crowbar anyway? It had flown from his hands when Dick punched him. He found it in the hands of a crazed man sitting on top of Scott. "Give us the water, you prick," the man said, and brought the crowbar down on Scott's face, which was briefly exposed under the pile of people. Something cracked, and blood shot from the bridge of Scott's nose before he disappeared under the pile again.

Got to save him, thought Cam, got to hurry. They're killing him, just like Jack. Even thinking hurt his head. Dick must have been holding something when he hit him. Something hard, because he definitely had a concussion.

Near the desk, Dick was pouring the water into his mouth, gulping it down so fast he was practically choking on it. The pile of punching arms and kicking legs was oblivious to it, and within seconds Dick had finished the whole jug by himself, spilling some of it onto his clothes.

Wasting it.

Cam felt his fists ball up, felt rage run down his spine. He wanted Dick dead. The man had already killed Jack, and now he was sealing Cobe's fate as well. But Scott was still under the pile and he had to save him, so Dick would have to wait. He tried to stand up again, and this time fought his way through the wooziness. First thing he did was kick out at the pile of people beating on Scott. The blow was weak, but his foot hit one man in the jaw and the man yelped and rolled off.

"Scott?" he yelled. "Get off him, you fuckers!" His brother-in-law was completely buried under the pile, just bits and pieces of him sticking out. One man swung a pipe, another swung a piece of metal that looked like it was torn off the trailer's side. All of them brought their weapons down on Scott.

"Scott?" No answer.

His head pounding and his vision blurry, Cam leapt on the pile and tried to pull the people off. He hooked his arms into the fray and yanked people back, put one man in a headlock before punching the man in the mouth. Every move hurt his head as if he was taking blows himself. Maybe he was; he was in so much pain it was hard to tell. One thing he did know: the pile was too strong to fight by himself. He was crying now, yelling for them to let Scott up, pleading for the life of his brother-in-law, telling them Scott didn't have any water. The people were desperate, thirsty, panicked. They kept swinging their weapons.

Someone grabbed Cam and locked him in a half nelson, immobilizing him, forcing him to watch as they beat Scott to death.

"Cam," came Scott's voice, feeble and distant. "Cam."

"Scott! Stopping hitting him, you fucks! Dick has the water! Dick has it!"

Nobody seemed to hear. For some reason they had singled Scott out as the man with the water, and they were still looking for it.

Scott's hand fell outward from under the pile again. In his palm lay the car keys, and Cam knew what it meant. He wouldn't let that happen. He couldn't. He threw his head back and slammed it into the nose of the man holding him. A flash of white erupted behind his own eyes, but the move freed him. The man fell away, but got right back up with a busted nose and went for Cam again. Cam leapt away, caught a glimpse of Scott's face under the pile—eyes swollen shut, nose broken, teeth missing.

Mr. Half-Nelson suddenly put a hand to his face and fell down.

Delayed reaction.

Dick was licking the inside of the jug, sitting under

the table like a child who'd just stolen a cookie.

"Cam . . . go . . . water . . . go," whispered Scott, right before a steel-toed boot caught him in the temple and burst his eyeball from the socket. Blood spread out beneath the heaving pile of pounding fists and feet. Scott's other eye rolled back in his head.

There was a scream that filled the trailer now; the scream of someone who'd just lost a friend and family member.

Nobody paid it much mind.

Mouth wide in anguish, Cam looked up at the lone jar of water on the shelves, the one Scott had left out of mercy, turned back and saw Dick looking at it as well. Shit, he'd drawn attention to it.

"Got more, huh?" Dick threw the empty jug aside and rushed the closet.

Cam tackled him, sending him to the floor, elbowed him in the head. Leaping over the pile, he grabbed the keys from Scott's hand before snatching the jar of water (which did not have a lid) from the shelf. He ran around the pile of people killing his brother-in-law and threw open the door.

Outside, the air kissed through his sweat-stained shirt and cooled him a bit, but it was still sweltering. He saw the ground around the observation well was already dry, and knew the water in the jar would soon be gone. The truck was unlocked when he reached it, a blessing since he wasn't sure which key unlocked it. He threw the keys in the ignition just as Dick and the crowd (many of them covered in Scott's blood) came rushing out at him.

He didn't think about what he did next.

Flooring the gas, he drove straight at them, one hand on the wheel, the other holding the jar of water. As crazy as the crowd was, they didn't want to die, and dove out of the way.

Except for one, the blonde girl he'd hit with the crowbar,

The truck bounced up over her body and spit her out the back where she went rolling into a cloud of dust.

When he was on the highway again, numbed by what he'd just done, he stuck a finger in the jar of water and licked it, felt his body shake with the need for more. No, it was for Cobe; he'd already had his jarful.

He drove in a daze for a little while, his head still reeling from the blow, his ears still ringing from screaming.

How would he tell Becky what had happened? She'd been through so much, anything more was just unfair. First her parents, and then her brother. Not to mention he'd cheated on her and broken her heart. How could he look her in the eyes and tell her Scott was dead, that he couldn't save him?

Part of him wanted to die right then and there as well. It would be easier than seeing the horror in her eyes when she found out. Easier than waiting for dehydration to take his life away, painful cramp by painful cramp. The other part of him knew he had to get this water home to her and Cobe before it disappeared. Paternal instinct, they called it. Or so he assumed.

Time was short. He had spilled some already, and the rest was down to about a half a cup.

Not enough to sustain life, but enough to prolong it.

The cramps in his gut came back stronger than ever, compounded by the guilt of not being able to save Scott. Eventually he put the jar between his legs and held his gut with his free arm.

At some point he turned the radio on, but all it played was news reports about the ocean receding. No one had an answer. This was followed by reports of people dying, mostly elderly, but some babies as well.

He cried the whole way home; his tears were thin and painful.

CHAPTER 17

The air conditioning in the house was no longer working. Becky didn't know much about that kind of thing but she was pretty sure the AC unit used some kind of liquid coolant, so that explained it. Anything with water in it. Ironically, sweat beaded on her upper lip, pooled under her arms, and ran down from her hair. Why did some waters evaporate faster than others? Why couldn't AC coolant be one of the slow ones?

An insatiable thirst was growing in her belly, and her head was starting to pound. It felt like the onset of a bad hangover. What the hell was going to happen to them, to her baby, if they didn't find water soon?

Scott would think of something though, he always did. He was the brains of the family, the scientist, the only one good with math. Scott said all the world's problems could be solved with science. As soon as he got back from finding Jack, he'd straighten everything out. He had to, right? Otherwise . . . no, she wouldn't dwell on it.

She looked at her watch, checked it against the wall clock to make sure it was correct. They'd been gone for almost two hours. Was that good or bad? She didn't know.

Turning away from the air conditioner, she went back over to the television where Cobalt lay on his blanket watching a children's DVD. She had turned the news off when they started showing dead bodies in the streets.

So quick, she had thought. Only two days without water and already people were dying. Some stations showed scenes from overseas, where the situation was the same, but most focused on America. All of them were talking about the ocean. For some reason, people were drinking the seawater. Or they had been, anyway . . . you had to walk out pretty far to get to the water now.

How does the ocean evaporate, she thought. It's just not possible. Only some kind of higher power could take away all the water on earth.

Instinctively, she thought of the crucifix hanging in the kitchen, the one that belonged to her mother. It took all of her strength not to go in there, yank it off the wall and throw it in the garbage.

"Sometimes God has to test our strength," her mother had told her when she was young. This was more than testing strength, though, this was impending death.

Still, she believed God was benevolent, and she wouldn't give in to the temptation to believe otherwise. Science might save them, but faith couldn't hurt.

She reached out and stroked her son's head, marveling at how soft his wisps of hair were. That's when she noticed his cranium looked odd, misshapen somehow. On closer inspection she saw that the baby's fontanel—the soft spot—was sunken in.

Panic seized her and she scooped him up. "Cobe!"

The baby came awake crying, startled from sleep.

She hated to set him off, but better she deal with his crying than find out he wasn't breathing; there were worse things than a baby's cry, and one of them most certainly was a baby's eternal silence. As she bounced him to calm him down, she played with his skin, shocked at how stretchy it had become. Dehydration was taking him away from her.

The smell hit her next, something beyond just a baby with a dirty diaper, something biologically foul. He has diarrhea, she realized, laying him down again so she could get a clean diaper.

Before she could get up, though, the door flew open and Cam rushed in, his face awash in blood, his shirt torn and stained red. In his hand he carried something that looked like—

"Water," he said, racing to her side. "Take a small drink. Hurry, before it goes away."

"There's hardly any," she said.

"Just do it. Then get Cobe's bottle."

She tipped the jar to her lips and felt the water soak into her dry tongue, slide down her throat and land like heaven in her stomach. Not too much, she thought, fighting back the urge to swallow it all; Cobe needed it more than her.

Unscrewing the lid of the baby's bottle, she poured the water in.

"Careful," Cam said. "Don't spill any."

"I can do it. Look out."

Picking up Cobe again, she thrust the bottle in his mouth and tipped the water toward the nipple. "Come on, Cobe, drink."

The baby wasn't drinking.

"Shit!" she screamed.

"Squeeze it," Cam said, "Push the water in his mouth."

"It's not that kind of bottle. It's hard plastic."

"Then take the damn top off and pour it in."

"Just let me do it!"

Cam backed off, his arm up in an okay-you-do-it gesture. She shouldn't have yelled, she realized, but she knew she had to do this herself, tense as it was making her. She was just about to take Cam's advice, dumb as it was, and squeeze the hard plastic bottle when Cobe finally began sucking on the nipple. Elation and relief flooded through her as the baby sucked in the water. Had Cam not held her and told her to relax, she wouldn't have even noticed she was shaking.

"What's wrong with his head?" Cam asked.

It wasn't that she didn't know the answer, she just didn't want to talk about it, and so said nothing.

When the water was gone, she changed the baby's diaper, saw there was hardly any waste. Her head spun, realizing he must be sick, not with diarrhea, but with dehydration and constipation. How she wanted to take him away from this slow torture. Dealing with diaper rash was bad enough, but watching him wither away . . . she would open her own veins and pour her blood into the baby's mouth if it would help.

It didn't even feel real when, for the first time that day, Cobe cooed and reached up toward her. When it sank in that he was happy, she cried and rocked him on the couch, ignoring the fact she could barely make tears.

He didn't look any different than he had a few minutes ago, though. His skin was still stretchy, his pigment slightly sallow, his head still oddly shaped.

Had Cam not shown up when he did, the situation could be worse.

If it could get worse.

"Hey, Cam . . . ?" Across the room, Cam looked up from the recliner where he sat, still covered in blood. She was about to thank him for the water, but instead said, "Where the hell is Scott?"

DAY FOUR

CHAPTER 18

There were no birds singing as Cam rolled off the couch, stumbled into the kitchen, and stopped at the sink. In fact there was little sound at all; no cars, no planes, no dogs barking or cats meowing. Nothing. His eyes were itchy and his stomach was thick with a dull ache. The concussion was keeping him dizzy, and he had to hold onto the edge of the counter to stay upright. It was worse now than it was last night.

"Come on, baby," he said, turning the faucet on.

The pipes knocked as air rushed through them, breathing a cloud of nothingness into the sink.

Still no water.

Oh God how the thirst was killing him.

Holding onto the counter, he walked over to the small television that sat near the microwave and turned it on. As the picture faded into view, he stepped over the broken pieces of the crucifix that lay on the floor, and made his way to the kitchen table. He sat down and looked at the jagged bit of Christ's head that lay near his foot. Becky had smashed it yesterday after he told her what had happened to Scott.

Since then, he hadn't seen her. She'd been locked in her room. No attempt to go in and console her had been successful. Even worse, she had left Cobalt in the living room. That was out of sorts for her. She never left Cobe for this long.

The baby had cried all night, sleeping on the floor next to the couch. When Cam opened his eyes this morning he could see his son's skin was drier, cracking at the joints, and the baby's eyes were sunken.

On the television, the first channel that swam into view showed only a station identification logo. The clock above the stove said it was past noon. (It wasn't rare for him to sleep this late, but rare enough for Becky.) How long had it been since he'd had any real liquid? How long since the newscasters had had any?

The remote was on the table, where Becky always kept it while feeding Cam. He switched channels until he found a local station that was live, a reporter standing in the middle of a vast desert. But it wasn't a desert, Cam soon learned by reading the caption at the bottom of the screen, it was one of the local beaches.

This was followed by a Presidential address, which was replayed on another channel as well. He hadn't known the President had given a speech; he'd been too busy dealing with Becky's grief and Cobe's crying last night to watch TV. The president, like everyone else, looked sickly. Liberals would be hard pressed to say the current administration was getting any special treatment. It was true: nobody had anything to drink.

He tried calling his parents and again got no answer. "Please be all right," he whispered. The last time he'd spoken to them was to inform them Becky had kicked him out and that he was staying with Joe. They'd asked why she'd done that but he didn't get into it.

Now, there was little else to do but sit at the table and wait for Cobe to wake up. He wondered if his son would eat the dried up food in the fridge (which was no longer working). Probably not. All the food in the fridge was dry as a bone. As was the air in the house; the inside of his nose was scaly and cracked, it was a wonder it wasn't bleeding.

Eventually the TV became mere background noise (how many times could he hear about the ocean disappearing and people keeling over?) and his thoughts drifted to Scott. Every time he closed his eyes he saw his brother-in-law lying under a pile of angry lunatics who were beating him to death.

Becky had blamed him, said he should have saved her brother.

She was right. He should have saved Scott. He was as worthless as Becky said he was.

Still, he had brought water to Cobe and that had to count for something. His love for his son wasn't just an act to impress Becky. It was rooted deep in his soul. He couldn't stand to see Cobe looking like this.

He also couldn't stand to see Becky so out of her mind. That wasn't an act either. Despite being back in the house with her, he still missed her terribly. How stupid he'd been to take her for granted. It seemed like just days ago they'd been going to bed together, saying I love you before they kissed and fell asleep in each other's arms. Sure, there'd been nights when they'd gone to bed angry, but those weren't worth thinking about right now.

What was worth thinking about was water. Specifically, the water in the trailer at the aquifer. How had Jack gotten so much water? There was no water tank nearby, and the small fridge was already open and tipped over when he and Scott had entered.

Where had the water come from? Why so many jars? If Jack had water, why not just pour it all into the jug in the first place. Why separate it? What was the white powder all over that pan that Scott had been so happy about?

"What was going on there, Scott. C'mon, man, just give me some kind of goddamn sign. I'm sorry about the Alanis Morissette thing."

For the next hour, he sat at the table hearing Scott's words over and over: the water has to go somewhere.

But where? And how had Jack gotten some?

The hours stretched into more hours. He measured time by how bad his insides felt.

Throughout the day, Cam moved only once, to change Cobe; the baby was ominously quiet, but there was little he could do. He tried spitting in a jar of dried baby food to moisten it, but Cobe wasn't having it. Couldn't blame him, really.

Becky never came out of her room, though he could hear her snoring from time to time. Best to let her rest.

For a long while he stared at Jesus' head on the floor.

The day erased itself.

The world continued to die.

It was as simple as that.

DAY FIVE

CHAPTER 19

Austin was on fire. A day ago nobody outside of Texas was giving Austin a thought, now it was all over the news, burning to cinders. The citizens had dug up the roads and planted homemade bombs along the water mains, sure that the government was blocking the water supply.

They'd missed the water pipes and hit the gas lines.

It was almost as bad as Boston, which was not only on fire, but without any civility whatsoever. Anyone suspected of having water was hanging by a noose from the nearest telephone pole. Survival now depended on how strong and crazy you were.

Chances were many other cities were facing the same problem. No one was banding together. This wasn't an outside threat like some terrorist attack by a fundamentalist group, this was mother nature against man. People were doing what they had to do to survive, to continue their very existences.

Trust was a word that no longer had meaning.

Cam knew all this from the handheld radio he kept on the kitchen table. The television stations had gone off late last night, so he'd dug around in Scott's room for the radio. It was a satellite version; leave it to a scientist to have the latest gadgets. In fact, a couple television stations still had camera feeds—live video from traffic cameras and whatnot—but there were no reports.

The Internet hadn't reported anything in a few hours either—at least the main websites like CNN and MSNBC hadn't. Lord knew some guy who spent his days whacking off to porn in his basement might still be blogging somewhere, but that meant little in the grand scheme of things.

Of all the stations on the radio, only a couple still had DJs talking. One was a Spanish speaking station, the other was an AM station Cam had never heard of. The man sounded old, gruff, weary—pissed off. He spoke slowly; clearly he had a sore throat, and more than once pontificated about the end of the world. Every so often he would report on something, but it was hard to tell where he was getting his information.

"Bedford residents have burned their town to the ground. The fires still rage. No water to put it out. You hear me, people? The devil has claimed us. All you adulterers, you drug addicts, and homosexuals . . . God is smiting us for your sins. John 4:14, people: 'But whosoever drinketh of the water that I shall give him shall never thirst.' But now we're all thirsting, aren't we? God is smiting us for your sins, you heathens. What's this? The hospitals in Providence have shut down. You hear that? No more medical help. The end of days, people, the end of days. Shit. Look at that, I'm cursing on the radio. Doesn't matter now. There ain't no FCC. All the feds are home hoarding their water supplies. Who wants to hear some Beach Boys?"

"Surfin' USA" blared from the radio and Cam had to turn it off or he'd end up throwing it across the room. God, he wished he was surfing now, oblivious to all the death unfolding around him. At least if he was out on the waves he wouldn't feel so goddamn alone.

Which reminded him, he hadn't spoken to Joe since seeing him at the pub.

When he dialed Joe's apartment a moment later he got no answer. Maybe he was out like the rest of the world, looking under rocks for puddles, breaking into stores in search of a juice carton that wasn't empty.

"I threw up."

He looked up and saw Becky standing in the doorway of the kitchen. It hurt to stand up as fast as he did, both from the concussion and the cramps in his stomach. He shoved the chair back and ran to her. This time she didn't shy away, but she didn't hug him back either.

"Are you okay?" he asked. Stupid question. Who the fuck was okay?

"I just said . . . I threw up. I'm sick."

She didn't need to say it for him to see it. Her face was pallid, her lips cracked, her weight was down. Despite this, and despite her breath stinking of vomit, he still wanted to kiss her. So he did.

She gave no reaction. Just stood there and let him do it.

"Come sit." He led her to the table.

"I saw Cobe in the living room, is he sleeping or dead?" She said it so matter-of-factly it stunned him.

"'Course he's not dead. He's sleeping. You think I wouldn't tell you if something happened to him?"

"Why not? Everyone else is dead. Everyone I care about is gone."

"I'm here. Don't you care about me?"

This time, when she didn't answer, he couldn't hold back his anger. "Jesus Christ, Becky, I'm here. I did my best. Look at me for a second. I got you water. And I'm fucking sorry already for what I did. I love you. Get it? I love you, and I'm here, so look at me like I'm a fucking human being, and say something nice because right now you're all I have, and I'm pretty sure I'm all you have, and we have a son in there who's going to die if we don't figure something out."

For the first time in two days, she looked in his eyes. "Figure what out, Cam? There's no more water and everyone's dead. The world is ending. I'm sick, you're sick, Cobe doesn't even cry anymore he's so sick. What can we figure out? Scott was the brains . . . and you let him—"

"Don't say it. Don't even fucking say it. I'd be dead too if Scott hadn't given me the okay to get out of there. That water I brought home, that would never have arrived if I'd stayed. Scott knew that. He gave his goddamn life for us so don't you sit here and dishonor that by locking yourself in your room and giving up. You hear me? He gave us a chance."

He fully expected her to slap him or chew him out or something, but she said nothing. They both sat in silence like that for a little while, listening to the floor creak.

"Where did you get the water?" Becky finally asked.

"I don't know. That professor friend of Scott's—"

"Jack?"

"Yeah . . . Jack."

"He dead?"

"Yeah. You knew him?"

"Not really. Scott said he was a nice guy, though."

"Ahhh!" The pain came out of nowhere and doubled Cam over in his chair. He groaned and grit his teeth as cramps thundered through his intestines. He'd been having them for several hours now, like the worst case of food poisoning he'd ever experienced. It took a minute, but it finally passed.

Becky was touching his shoulder, he could feel her hand there. When he sat back up she took it away. Maybe he'd finally gotten through to her with his little speech. After all, they were going to have to be a team to get Cobe some water. The thought of her warming up to him gave him a jolt of hope, but he didn't say anything; better to let the moment stand.

"Cramps?" she asked. "Me too."

"God, that one hurt."

"Good. Now you know how it feels when your husband cheats on you."

Okay, so maybe she wasn't warming up exactly; maybe she just realized she needed him to survive.

"The water?" she said, as if to remind him where they'd left off.

"Right, the water. Jack had all these jars of water in a storage closet. He also had this pan with this white stuff and Scott seemed to think he'd figured something out but I don't know what it was."

"He didn't say?"

"He was about to. He'd just dipped his hand in it and . . ."

A thought fluttered into Cam's woozy head. He let it sit there for a moment trying to digest it, like working out a math problem. Becky asked him if he was okay, waved a hand in front of his face.

He ignored her and went and got Scott's car keys off the counter. "He touched the keys."

"So?"

Cam flipped them around, studying the UCSD keychain on them. There, right on the logo, was what he was looking for. The white powder. From Scott's hand, no doubt. He smelled it, just like Scott had done, but couldn't discern an odor. Was it a chemical?

Tentatively, he licked it.

"It's salt," he said.

Becky got up from the table, ambled over next to him and looked at the keychain. "Some of the aquifers drill up salt water. Scott tells me . . . used to tell me . . . but it bores me so I don't listen much."

"Jack was at that salt water aquifer. The ocean is evaporating slower than everything else."

"Which all means what? You're not supposed to drink ocean water. Even I know that."

"Scott said something about third grade science."

"Did you pass third grade?"

He looked up at her and smiled. "Well well well, Becky's back."

"I wasn't kidding."

He let the snide comment slide and got back to thinking about the salt. "How can you get the salt out of the water? Or better yet, how do you get the water out, leaving the salt behind? Jack got the clean water out and into the jars somehow."

They both stood there thinking for some time, until finally Cobe woke up and made a noise. Becky gave up and went to check on him.

Cam stared at the floor and said, "Shit. Why am I not smart enough to figure this out?"

Another cramp slammed through his insides and he doubled over once more, sure he was going to die right there. Oh God, it hurt. The pain was the worst yet, spiked with heat and bubbling, the acid in his stomach like lava in a volcano.

When the pain finally passed, he stood back up . . .

. . . and saw Joe staring at him through the kitchen window. "Joe?"

"Give us some water, Cam," Joe said.

What the hell was he talking about?

Behind Joe, at least a hundred people stood on the lawn, all of them looking in through the window at Cam. All of them held some kind of weapon. A couple of them even had rifles.

One of the people was Dick.

Without thinking, Cam yelled, "Becky, lock the door!"

CHAPTER 20

Becky appeared in the kitchen entryway with Cobalt in her arms when the pounding started on the front door. It slammed on its hinges, shaking the front of the house, but didn't open.

It was already locked, thank God.

Becky cried out and ran to Cam. "What the fuck is that?"

Through the window, Cam looked at Joe. His friend's face was sickly, the same stretchy skin and cracked lips as the rest of the world. There was desperation in his eyes coupled with a panic unlike anything Cam had ever seen. "We don't have water," Cam said.

"He has water," Dick yelled. "They had a whole jar of it at the trailer. I saw it."

Cam wanted to go outside and kill Dick, smash his head in somehow. Here was the guy who'd masterminded the fatal beating of Becky's brother, the guy who would have killed Cam too if he'd caught him. The guy deserved a slower death than he was already getting. Only the guns out there were keeping Cam from doing anything stupid.

"Jesus, Cam, if you have water you gotta share it with us." Joe's palms were flat against the window pane, trying to raise the glass.

"What are you doing here, Joe?" Cam reached out and latched the window closed. The front door banged again as someone gave it another kick.

"Everyone in the whole damn city knows you have water. That guy saw you with it." Joe pointed to Dick. "Is it true?"

"What's he talking about?" Becky asked.

Cam saw the sudden fear in her eyes, saw the baby in her arms and felt terrified and angry all at once. What if these psychos tried to hurt his kid like they'd done to Scott?

He suddenly remembered Scott saying something about shooting his father's gun. It had to be in the house somewhere. Keeping his voice low, he asked Becky where it was.

"It's in Scott's bedroom, in his closet, I think."

Bang! The door shook again. *Bang!*

"C'mon, Cam," Joe said, still trying to get the window open. "I gave you a place to stay, just give me some water. Fair is fair."

"You kicked me out, Joe."

"Yeah, well, you should see the mold in my bathroom. And I still got your hair everywhere and . . . just give us some goddamn water or they're going to kill you, you fucking asshole!"

Mold, thought Cam. With that, the final piece of the salt water equation fell into place.

"Oh, my God," he said, turning to Becky. "I think I know how Jack did it."

Becky was trembling, holding Cobe in her arms like she was trying to jam him inside her body to protect him. "What? How?"

"Simple . . ." He looked back at Joe, was about to tell him the secret, but stopped when he saw Dick pressed up against the window.

"Hi, shithead," Dick said, right before swinging an ax into the glass.

Cam yanked Becky down as the window exploded. Tiny glass daggers fell to the floor around them like a death rain. Instantly, he could hear the mob rush the house and start pounding on the walls. The whole place shook like it was at the epicenter of an earthquake. The mob was so loud, so bloodthirsty, Cam had to yell over their war cries to hear himself.

"Becky! Get the gun! Hurry! Go!"

Still holding Cobe, Becky ran down the hall to Scott's room, damn near hysterical as she went.

Cam grabbed a butcher knife from the knife holder on the counter. As Dick grabbed the windowsill to hoist himself up and in, Cam rammed the knife down hard. The blade stabbed through the tendons in Dick's hand, pinning him to the sill. The man screamed bloody murder, but it gave Cam a second to breathe.

He needed three things: A pot, its lid, and a lighter.

He found the pot and lid in one of the cabinets near the stove, ran into the living room and jammed them inside Scott's backpack, which still sat on the couch from two days ago.

"Becky!"

From down the hall: "Oh my God, Cam!"

"Lighter! Where's a lighter!"

"Lighter?"

"Yes, lighter! A fucking lighter! Where is one!"

She came running out of the room, Cobe in one arm and the rifle in the other. She was haphazardly carrying bullets in the same hand as the gun.

Cam suddenly realized she was wearing only her bathrobe and pajamas. He himself was barely dressed in just his boxer shorts and a t-shirt. Neither was wearing shoes.

"There's a lighter in that drawer there." She pointed to a cabinet near the front door, which was shaking fiercely in its frame. He grabbed the lighter from the drawer and threw it in the bag. Next, he ran into the kitchen (Dick still groaning at the window), got the satellite radio and added that to their supplies.

"Get behind me," he said, and took the gun from her hand.

"I'm not letting them touch, Cobe. I'll fucking kill them."

He raised the gun at the door just as an ax cut through its center (just like in that Kubrick movie, he thought). A hand reached through and undid the latch, and suddenly Joe was there, his chest rising and falling with adrenaline. Cam cocked the rifle. "Back up, Joe."

"Please, Cam, we just want a drink. We're dying."

"We're all dying."

From behind Joe, someone screamed out to "Shoot the fucker and take the water." People started piling into the house. One of them raised a gun at Cam, but thankfully didn't shoot.

From behind him, Cam heard people coming through the sliding glass door that led to the back yard.

They were surrounded.

"We're leaving, Joe. I don't want to shoot you but I will. I've got a backpack here. Nothing else. I'll show you what's in it."

Joe said nothing, not quite sure what to make of this.

"Becky, open the pack."

Still holding Cobe—who was suffering from the lethargic effect of the dehydration—she opened the pack and leaned it toward Joe.

"See," Cam said, "nothing in there but a pot and radio. Nothing on us unless you feel like sticking your hand in my ass and checking."

Joe shook his head.

"The house is yours," Cam continued. "Search around if you think we have water. We're leaving. The first man who gives us a problem gets shot. We're all dying, Joe . . . do me a solid, okay? Let us leave and die in peace."

For a second it looked like Joe and his cohorts might leave, but instead they fanned out through the house, tearing it apart. One of them was wearing a policeman's uniform.

Grabbing Becky, Cam led them outside, listening to the destructive noises coming from the house, the sound of civilization seeping further into hell. When he looked around, he gasped. He hadn't been outside in over a day, and didn't really know how bad it had gotten.

Everything was dead.

Everything.

The trees, the plants, all of it brown. No more lawn. No more leaves. Dead animals littered the road. Some skeletal corpses lay on a neighbor's lawn. There were no birds singing. Cars were parked wherever they'd died. The sky was void of clouds, the sun fiery and oppressive.

"Jesus," he whispered.

A grunting sound caught his attention and he turned to see Dick still stuck to the window sill, trying to yank the knife from his hand. His face was blistered and pocked with bleeding pustules. His mouth was a mass of dried blood and open fissures.

"Hi, Dick," he said. "How's that salt water treating you?"

Dick turned, saw Cam watching him. He stopped struggling and said, "Go on, shoot me. You think I care? It's better than this."

"I'm not gonna shoot you," Cam said. "I'm gonna torture you."

"What?"

"What?" Becky said as well, still frantic to get Cobe to safety.

"Not like that, Dick. Not with pain. With this: knowledge. I know where to get drinking water. Jack knew it too, and I bet you a million fucking dollars he would have explained it to you had you just asked. But you didn't ask, you greedy fuck. You just decided to kill him, like you did Scott."

Becky gasped and managed to get in a powerful punch to Dick's eye before Cam put out a hand and held her back. "So I'm going to leave now, and you'll never find us, and we'll be drinking water while you die a slow death stuck to my window. That's your torture."

Dick's eyes went wide, and just as he started to

scream, no doubt to inform everybody of what Cam had just said, Cam smashed the butt of the gun into his nose and knocked him clean out.

CHAPTER 21

They'd been driving for a while and Becky's arms, supporting the baby, were hurting. Cobe hadn't made a sound in a long time, and that was scaring her to death. Some kind of made-up prayer had been rolling off her lips for several minutes: "You're my precious baby and we'll play in the playground soon. You're my precious baby and we'll play . . . "

It hurt her throat just to talk.

She pressed her ear against the baby's chest to make sure he was still alive, and found herself crying when she felt his breath. The sobs came out in gigantic gasps.

She was losing it, and she knew it. It was more concerning that she was starting not to care.

Next to her, Cam looked over but didn't say anything.

"How much farther?" she asked, trying to regain her composure. Outside her window, a large marine mammal lay dead and dry in the sand. Some kind of whale; she wasn't any good with that stuff. Scott had loved the Discovery Channel but she was a gossip show kind of person. Whatever it was it looked big, with sharp teeth and large black eyes. She'd have hated to meet it in the water.

Back when there was water in the Pacific Ocean

Next to her, staring through the dirty windshield,

Cam pointed straight ahead and answered. "Until we find it," he said.

And then the SUV died. Just like that.

Just like everything else was doing.

Dying.

"That was a long way for fumes," Cam said. His voice was slow and strained. His mouth was hurting him. "We got lucky. Real lucky."

"Oh God, Cam, it's fucking starting to hurt."

"Me too. Gotta keep moving, though. Gotta find the water."

Getting out of the SUV, Cam took two bicycles off the roof and put them on the sand. He'd found them at an abandoned house on the way to the beach. Thankfully the SUV had a bike rack (Dick, Joe, and the rest of the Loose Screw Brigade had slashed the tires on his own car and snapped his surfboard in half so he'd had little choice but to take Scott's vehicle). He opened the backpack, added some tools from the trunk and some dead tree branches he'd picked up, and slipped it on.

"Come on," he said. "We've got to keep going. We've got to stay ahead of it."

She was about to rebut when she was suddenly racked with intense cramps, nearly dropping Cobe as she bent forward and grunted. Cam was on it, grabbing the baby from her arms. She bent over and dry heaved into the dirt for several minutes. Her insides screamed with *need*... need for water. For any kind of liquid that would satisfy her body's withered, dry cells. When it passed, she stood sucking in air like a hooked fish in a boat until she could walk again.

"I'll hold the baby," Cam said, climbing onto one of the bikes.

As she got on the other bike, she saw the baby was limp in Cam's arms. "I don't want you to hold him," she said.

"What?"

"Give me my baby! You don't get to hold him! You don't even love me!" She wasn't quite sure where this was coming from, but it had been in her for a while and it seemed to take control. This man, this person whom she'd loved—still loved—had ripped her heart out and now wanted to take her baby and carry him around like a rag doll. He wasn't a rag doll, he was her creation. Her life. Her little Cobe whose heart was still pure and innocent. She wouldn't let Cam destroy her baby. Cobe wasn't going to leave her because of Cam's stupidity.

Right?

Maybe she was wrong. She felt so dizzy, she didn't know what was what anymore. All she knew was that the lifeless form in Cam's arms was not her Cobe. Her Cobe was a giggling, cooing, crying little boy; he most certainly did not hang limp.

"Don't drop him," Cam said, giving her back the baby.

She snatched the boy out of his arms and cradled him close, felt his heart beating against her eardrum. The sound echoed through the pounding headache she was fighting.

"You cool now?" Cam asked.

She didn't know. What did cool mean, anyway? Could cool exist in their circumstance? Did cool exist in someone like Cam, with his face all white and . . .

Jesus. It was as if she was noticing his features for the first time in days. Face gaunt,

eyes sunken, lips covered in dried blood from where they'd split, his skin loose around his neck like a turkey's waddle.

Did she look the same way? Did everyone who was still alive look that way?

Was anyone still alive? Cam had turned the radio on in the car for a bit but every station hissed with dead air.

"You got him?" Cam asked, referring to the baby.

She nodded yes and started pedaling.

Together, they rode further out into the desert that was once the Pacific Ocean. Riding the bike in the sand was not easy, and it made her muscles flare with exertion. She held Cobe in one arm and maneuvered with the other. Fortunately, the slope of the ground fell downward in their direction and for the most part she just had to steer. Sometimes the sand got real thick and she had to walk the bike through it. She tried to stay on top of all the dead fish and dry seaweed as much as possible. It was like riding on a bad cobblestone road.

The baby bounced and jostled in her arm as she pedaled, his head flopping about whenever she hit a dip or small hill. More than once Cam asked if he could hold the baby. She told him no.

Something large loomed on the horizon. She asked Cam what it was but he said he didn't know. "Might be an oil tanker," he said after a while, "or a cruise ship of some kind."

It was a while before they passed the first sail boat,

the *Lucky Lady*. It sat lopsided in the sand, its sail pointed up at an angle toward the sinking sun, four corpses lying on the sand around it. Their faces were mummified. "They probably drank the seawater," Cam said.

She would drink it too if they happened on to any—which was the plan.

As the slope continued to lead them down, her ears began to pop, and the headache that had begun so long ago seemed to drive nails into her nerves. Time stopped having meaning, and she kept count of their journey by measuring the weirdness of the dead, dry fish that littered the ground. There were thousands of them. No, millions.

"Shark," Cam said at one point.

A scream escaped her mouth before she realized she was making it. The shark lay on its side, its mouth ringed with the kind of fangs she thought only existed in nightmares. It was so goddamn huge.

"Can't believe I used to surf with that thing in the water."

"Is it dead?"

Cam got off his bike, walked over to the large creature and put a hand against its torpedo-shaped body, right above the dorsal fin. "Dry as paper," he said. From the backpack he took a small screwdriver he'd found in the car's trunk and jammed it into the beast's side, cut out a chunk of flesh. He smelled it first, then deciding it was ok, he ate it. "S'like eating Ritz crackers. You want any?"

Was he nuts? Eat that thing? It was grotesque. She

still couldn't get over how huge it was, at least 25 feet judging on how it measured up next to Cam. Blood stained its teeth and the white skin under its snout.

He spit the rest out, perhaps realizing it wasn't so good after all, and they continued their descent.

The fish got weirder, larger, more grotesque, with odd shapes and huge bulging eyes. They passed some dolphins, a graveyard of hammerhead sharks, and the largest whale she'd ever seen. Cam said it was a humpback.

All of them were dead.

For a little while she even forgot about the lifeless form in her arms, but when the baby's eyes fluttered she leapt off the bike and cried out. Cam was beside her in an instant.

"What? What's wrong?"

"Cobe's eyes! Look!"

The baby's eyes fluttered open and closed a few times, rapidly, involuntarily, and finally came to rest half open. His eyeballs rolled back in his head, his irises disappearing under the lids. His little mouth, cracked and dry, fell open. His head, its fontanel sunken in like a bowl, convulsed a few times while his legs kicked.

Then Cobe went silent.

And in Becky's mind, everything followed suit.

CHAPTER 22

The breeze blew over the sand, over the dead sea creatures and over the three figures crouched low on the sea floor. A ghostly howl seemed to rise in pitch for several minutes, carrying sand and salt through the air like confetti raining down on the saddest party ever thrown. The wail that accompanied it began slowly, emanating from some place deep and guttural, rising to a crescendo that shook the soul of earth.

A supreme numbness washed over Cam as he reached out and closed his little boy's eyes forever. Every ounce of his being wanted to look skyward and curse God, but he held back, concerned for the woman that was burying her head into the baby's dead body. His wife.

It took a while before Becky looked up again, her face red and thin, her eyes hollow and tinged with yellow.

"Becky," he said, touching her shoulder. "Becky, he's gone."

"No he's not!" she screamed.

"He is. And we can't stay here, we have to keep going."

"To what," she screamed. "To where? There's nothing Cam, there's no water left."

"Yes there is. There has to be. There was the day

before we left so some of the ocean has to still be here. We haven't gone deep enough."

Her emotions switched from anger to defeat, and she began to rock back and forth. "Don't want to go," she said. "Just leave me with my baby. Not going."

"We could . . . maybe we should . . . " He was going to suggest they bury Cobe but couldn't bring himself to actually say it. Instead, he relied on just nodding toward the baby, hoping she'd understand him.

"No," she said. "He's my baby. He stays with me."

The reality of the moment began to settle in as he looked at his dead son's face. Dead. Gone. Forever. He was suddenly overcome with sobs, though not a single tear fell from his eyes. He choked on his grief, then forced himself to be strong again. "We can't take him," he said.

"He's my baby," Becky said. "I'm not leaving him."

There was no arguing with her, that much he could see. She was somewhere inside her own mind, someplace happier than where they actually were. It broke his heart, but if they planned on living they had to get to water soon.

"Please, Becky,"

"Fuck you, Cam! Don't you touch my baby!"

He threw his hands in the air, backed off a bit. "Okay, Beck. Okay, you hold Cobe. But we have to ride. Can you ride?"

"I don't want to."

Taking a risk, he put his arms around her and hugged her close, noting how skinny she felt. Even though the bathrobe, her knobby bones jutted into his own.

She didn't back off like normal, didn't scream or yell or insult him. What she did was lay her head on his shoulder for a minute and say, "I'm thirsty. How much farther is it?"

"Close, Beck, I'm telling you we have to be close. But we have to hurry. Are you going to come now?"

Her moods were on some kind of shuffle program, because she stood up and got back on the bike, said, "Let's go."

"Are you taking Cobe?"

"Yes. And don't you try to take him, okay. Let's just get some water. Maybe he'll feel better if we get him some water."

Cam let the comment fade out into the empty seabed, got on his bike, and started to pedal down the slope before them.

He looked back once to make sure Becky was still following. She stared off into space as she rode, the baby hanging unnaturally in her arm.

They passed another whale, some large fish with big noses, and saw another ocean liner in the distance, sticking out of the ground like a monolith. Occasionally, crabs skittered over the dead creatures, yanking off the dried flesh and doing their best to eat it. There was plenty to go around, that was for sure. All that bullshit he'd heard about people fishing the oceans dry was a crock; there were more dead things lying on the ground now than if every fish market in the world piled their stock together. Many of the fish were so big they could feed small nations. At one point, Cam's bike tire rolled over an octopus and tangled it up in the spokes. Thankfully, the tentacles were brittle enough that they snapped off after a few rotations.

Eventually, he smelled the water.

The salty scent was an uppercut to his fuzzy head, and he cried out to Becky, who seemed uninterested in anything except looking at the tiny body pressed against her breasts.

"Water, Becky. I told you!"

No reply.

He used his feet to push the bike along as fast as he could, checking back once or twice to make sure she was following. It was twenty minutes before they came upon the chasm that cut through the sea floor. The gigantic fissure in the earth's crust hid a bottom that was shimmering.

Water.

CHAPTER 23

It took the better part of the night to get down to the bottom of the chasm, mostly because they had to keep stopping for Becky to deal with Cobe. She too, at least, seemed urged on by the smell of water. Thankfully they'd hit the giant crack at a point where it sloped up to meet the sea floor, so the climb down was maybe only three stories. Still, it was fairly steep.

When they reached the bottom, they found themselves standing in water up to their ankles. It felt too good to believe, and Cam had to fight the urge to just slurp it up.

"We have to hurry," he said. "It's already disappearing. I can see it going down."

Nearby, Becky swayed in the hot night air, her body so emaciated she looked like a reedy piece of seaweed in an underwater diorama. "Peel some meat off that fish over there," Cam said, pointing to what looked like some kind of angler fish still flapping on a small rise of dirt. It was good to see the animal alive.

Becky stomped it dead with her foot and clawed a chunk of meat off its back, dark blood running down her fingers.

"Eat it," Cam told her.

She ate, which, really, was a testament to their destitution, because Becky was a pretty picky eater most of the time. She wolfed it down, tore another piece off and ate that one as well. The whole time she tore at the fish, she held the dead baby in her arms.

"Whoa, save me some."

"Here." She gave him a piece and he wolfed it down. It was still moist, though much of it tasted like salt water and that was something they needed to avoid.

Laying the dead branches from the backpack on an area jutting out from the chasm wall, Cam lit a small fire, jury-rigged a make-shift oven range over it with some rocks, and put a pot of seawater on it.

"Moment of truth. How smart was Jack?" He scooped the seawater up into the jar, set the jar in the pot, and put the lid over the whole thing.

"What's that gonna do?" Becky asked.

She looked at Cobe and cooed to him, and Cam knew for sure she was someplace else, someplace where the baby was giggling and watching *Sesame Street*.

"It's what Jack knew. What Scott knew. It's goddamn third grade education. Condensation. You boil any liquid and put a cover on it, the steam sticks to the lid. It leaves the salt behind. Same way you get mold in a bathroom. The steam rises, leaves water droplets on the ceiling. At least I hope."

The next two minutes were the longest two minutes in the existence of Cameron's life. When he took the lid off the pot, the moonlight illuminated beads of water like tiny diamonds. He tilted the lid and let it pool in the thin rim.

Cam licked it.

Water. Fresh, drinkable, water.

"Hurry," he told Becky, and she staggered forward and licked the lid as well. Her eyes rolled back in her head and she tasted the sweet, salt-free liquid.

"Give some to Cobe," she said. "He needs some."

"Becky . . ."

"C'mon. Don't waste it."

An extreme pathos cut through him as he wet his finger with the water and rubbed it across his dead son's cracked, dry lips. Of course, the baby didn't move, but Becky didn't seem to mind. She merely smiled at the boy's blue face and hugged him close, said, "That's my boy. Everything's going to be all right."

Fighting back tears that probably wouldn't form anyway, Cam scooped up another jar of water and turned the satellite radio on.

It was silent.

LAST DAYS

CHAPTER 24

By morning, the sun was back out fully recharged, the air a blanket of invisible flame that tore through their skin and gave rise to white blisters and red welts.

The water was gone. All of it. Poof. Like that. They'd drunk (or licked, to be more precise) what they could throughout the night, trying to beat the rapidity of its disappearance, but the water faded before their eyes. Now, the sea floor was littered with seaweed, dead fish and crustaceans (all dry as bone) and a whole lot of salt that stung their open sores.

Cam lay on his back, staring up at the blue sky, ignoring the pain of the salt on his exposed skin, listening to his wife breathing slowly next to him. The baby, its skin a light gray hue, lay on top of her chest, rising and falling on her body as her lungs fought for oxygen.

He could not bring himself to look at the boy's face.

There were so many things he wanted to ask the sky, but could not find the strength. Mostly just . . . Why? Why Earth? Why the people? What had they done wrong? Was it God's choice? Had science had something to do with it all?

Why now, when he'd seen the error of his ways, when he knew, more than anything, that he wanted to do right by his son?

Why?

The water, refreshing as it had been, had done little to revive him or Becky. He hadn't even urinated yet. Any precious fluids were sweating out from his scalp. He wore only his boxers and T-shirt, the rest of his body exposed to the sun like a fast food burger under a heat lamp.

Words kept rolling around inside his mind—Scott's words: the water has to go somewhere. But it hadn't. It hadn't gone anywhere except away. Drawn from everything on the planet as far as he could tell. Taking life away with it. Some lives faster than others, but all life in the end.

Where had the water gone?

Beside him, Becky groaned. She had stretched out first about an hour ago, sick to her stomach, aching and dizzy, talking to Cobe like it was just any other normal day.

He'd tried to get her up, but soon realized the futility of it. She wasn't going to move. She probably *couldn't* move.

He saw the futility of everything else as well—trying to find more water, walking across the dry sea floor, pushing himself harder than his body could take. They'd bought a tiny bit of time with what they'd drunk, but not much.

Enough, perhaps, to finally rest and be together.

"Becky," he whispered. She grunted and lolled her head sideways to look at him. Her tongue was swollen, her jaw bone thin, the gums receding around her teeth.

"I'd have changed. I swear it. I know I hurt you, real bad, and I'm sorry."

She blinked, said nothing.

"I love you," he said, knowing for once what the weight of those words really meant. "Oh God, I love you."

It was a slow movement on her part, but she laid her hand out for him, and he took it. They held hands as the sun climbed higher in the sky.

CHAPTER 25

There was an Eighth Day, which passed without movement or sound, and eventually fell into darkness.

CHAPTER 26

On the Ninth Day, the sky turned gray, then green, then black, and with a low rumble that sounded like an old man waking up, a single raindrop fell onto the three lifeless bodies that lay in an eternal embrace in the trench cutting across the ocean floor.

Another drop followed.
And another.
And another.

GOPHERS

a short story

RAY THREW A shovelful of dirt into the open green trash bin, wiped sweat from his forehead. "Hey, thanks for helping me do this, Quinn. I mean it."

"No sweat," Quinn replied. "This type of problem, it's everyone's problem. If we don't all band together there won't be a single rose bush left in the whole neighborhood. Gophers are like a virus--you don't cut 'em out quick they just spread. Speaking of which, how do you like the neighborhood so far?"

"Love it. Couldn't be happier. Just the fact you and Benito came over the other day to welcome me says volumes. I've lived in a lot of places the last few years and never had a neighbor so much as wave. When I was growing up, I knew everyone on my street."

Quinn rested on his shovel for a moment, bent over and picked up his beer from the ground. He took a long swig and let out a sigh of relief. "Tell me about it. It's like people forgot how to be friends. It's all social media and cell phones these days. My daughter . . . " He trailed off, let his words form into a smile. Then, "well, you know, kids and computers."

"I'll have to take your word for it."

"No kids?"

"No. My ex and me tried. It didn't take. Just as well, she went and fucked her mechanic. She was a whore."

"Sorry to hear that. That why you moved into this house? New start?"

Ray looked up at the two story, white stucco house he'd just put a first and last month's rental deposit on. It needed work and was definitely the biggest eyesore on the street, but he'd told the owner he was handy and would help fix it up if I could move in quickly; the hotel he'd been staying in had had a pest problem of its own: gangbangers and teenage prostitutes. The stucco was falling off in some areas, and the pergola was leaning so far to the right it ought to be wearing a Rush Limbaugh shirt. But the biggest problem was the collection of dirt mounds in the front and back yards. Gophers had taken up residence under the soil and destroyed what had once been a collection of orange and lemon trees, as well as about two dozen rose bushes.

"You could say that," Ray said. "Plus I always wanted to live in California. Your wife cheating on you and ripping your heart out is one thing, but shoveling snow out of your driveway at six in the morning for nine months might be the bigger bitch."

Quinn laughed, dug his shovel in the ground again. "I hear you. Don't get any snow here. Where you from then?"

"Jersey. And before you ask, yes it's true what they say. It's a shithole."

"Ooh! Found a tunnel. C'mere."

Ray made his way over to the long trench now cutting through the backyard. He could see two small black holes on either side of it, like passageways in a sewer system. "Well lookie at that. Never actually seen one before, you know. We don't have them on the East Coast. Least not where I'm from."

"That's the fucker's hallway right there," Quinn said. He made his way back to the patio, grabbed two of the black box traps he'd brought over, carried them back to the holes. He set the trigger mechanism on each and placed one against each hole. "That's the trick," he said. "You gotta block both holes. No way to tell if the little shit is near the fence or in the middle of the yard. Their tunnel system can get pretty intricate. They've got main sleeping chambers and food storage rooms and main tunnels and tunnels that branch off in twenty different directions. Bastards even have a bathroom set up. They're not cute, dancing fluffs like in fucking *Caddyshack*. They're a goddamn menace."

"Must be a rite of passage out here to catch these things."

"You have no idea. They'll ruin your whole yard ten times over in a season. My daughter used to say I was obsessed. First thing in the morning I'm out checking the traps. I get home from work I'm out checking the traps. 'Dad, you need a new hobby,' she used to say."

"Cute. How old is your daughter?"

"She would have been nineteen last month."

It took only a second for Ray to realize he was staring like an idiot. But what was a man supposed to say to a bombshell like that? You just don't ask a man you've only known for three days how and why he lost his daughter. So of course he made it worse by stammering. "I . . . uh . . . "

"It's fine," Quinn said. "I see it in your eyes. I don't tell you someone else on the street will. She left one night with her boyfriend, Mike, off to see a movie. Three years ago. She never came back. A month later they found Mike's car in Mexico. Cops say it was anything from a drug deal gone bad to a carjacking. My baby girl didn't do drugs and I actually liked Mike. He was a nice kid. His parents moved a few months ago. Couldn't stay here anymore. Went to Colorado. Anyway, the police and FBI searched for over a year. Nothing. Mexican police, well, you'll find out soon enough you go down there. They only move if you give them American dollars, but the problem is they also lie out their ass. So I paid them half my life's savings only to finally catch on they weren't investigating shit for me."

Ray spoke before he could even stop himself. "Maybe she's still—"

"Alive? No. She ain't. Trust me. You're not from here. Mexican gangs get you, you don't go home again. Maybe, if there'd been a ransom, then yeah, she'd probably have come back just missing a finger or two. But those sick fucks don't care about human life. They're animals. I know she's dead, buried somewhere in a shitty town full of cockroaches and mule shit. She's gone. And for what? A car? The twenty bucks I gave her for popcorn? Fuck." A tear rolled down Quinn's eye and he dropped the shovel, bent over and grabbed his beer again.

Not for the first time Ray saw the deep lines in Quinn's face. The black rings around his eyes. The silver hair that probably should still be brown on top. It was as if the man had cried all the color out of his life.

"I'm sorry," Ray said, feeling stupid. He'd cried after his divorce, but he could not imagine this type of pain.

Quinn pointed at the holes. "Don't be. Not your fault. Life sucks and you deal with it. C'mon, we have a bead on his tunnel now so we need to set more traps. I always dig a circle around the yard to see if they're going under the fence into the neighbor's yard. Like I said, this is a neighborhood effort. Tell you what, I'll do the circle and you dig this way, along the sprinkler line. They like to be near the pipes for some reason." He pointed his hand at an angle back toward the patio. "If you spot the holes I'll show you how to set the trap."

With a nod, Ray took one more pull off his beer and tossed the empty bottle into the blue recycling bin near the pergola. He set about digging a trench in the direction Quinn instructed. It was grueling work in the hot sun. The back of his neck was burning and sweat was running down his arms. He'd been told San Diego wasn't humid but whoever had spouted that fact had been wrong.

He'd gone about eight feet when he found the telltale black tunnel holes of the gopher. "Bingo."

Quinn, who had made quick time with his digging, rushed over and showed Ray how to lock the trigger mechanism on the black box and secure them properly.

"How many you catch with these," Ray asked.

"Oh, shit, dozens. They work. You don't have dead gophers by the morning I'll eat the dirt we're digging up."

"Bold statement."

"I'm a bold man. I taught Benito across the street, too. Which reminds me, when we're done here we need to do the front yard. They can tunnel under the street and hit Benito's house easy as pie. We'll set traps out front too."

"The front yard already looks pretty bad. Guess it won't make it any worse."

"Don't worry about aesthetics, Ray, everyone on the street does it. You want green grass, you gotta get under the dirt first and kill these fuckers."

The sun was directly overhead now, and Ray wondered how much longer they'd have to dig trenches. Half the yard now looked like a miniature of the Western Front, 1916 . "Want another beer?" was all he could ask.

Quinn just smiled. "Does the pope shit in the woods?"

• • •

AFTER FOLLOWING QUINN'S instructions for digging a few more trenches through the center of the backyard, complete with six more traps set, they moved to the front yard and got to work. Thankfully the front lawn was much smaller, and Quinn suggested just making a couple quick cuts through the middle and then one around the edge near the curb. Over the next hour they set four more traps and filled the remaining two yard barrels with dirt, which they both hauled onto the side of the house.

"Now what?" Ray asked. His back ached, he was

starving and his legs were near to wobbling.

Quinn raised and shook his empty beer bottle, his fourth of the day. "Now we drink more and wait for dusk. They're most active around sunset."

"Oh, don't feel like you have to stay to do *that*. I feel bad you've been here so much today as it is. I can come out and check them in a few."

"Nonsense. It's not like I have much else to do. I don't talk to you, Ray, I'm just gonna talk to my goldfish. And them fuckers ain't much for conversation. And truth be told I don't get out much. Unless you want me to go."

Well I'd like to take a nap, thought Ray, but I supposed it'd be rude to turn away a helpful neighbor, especially one who's got such deep emotional wounds. "Not at all," he said. "I'll grab another round for us."

• • •

THEY SAT ON the front porch in two kitchen chairs Ray hauled out. They sipped their beers and watched the sun get lower, though it didn't do much to the blazing hot winds drying up the last of the grass. A few pickups drove by the house and disappeared up and over a nearby hill. Some teens skateboarded by going the other way, and Ray saw Quinn's head dip a little. How hard it must be, Ray thought, to never know what happened to your kid.

He pointed at Quinn's shirt, which showed a volcano and some palm trees. The words Kilauea, Hawaii were stenciled under it. "You go to Hawaii much?"

"Never been. My daughter bought this for me when she went with her school band years ago. She played the flute."

"Shit. Sorry. "

"It's fine. A man's gotta get on living. I did do a bunch of travelling not long ago, though. Figured I owed it to myself to get out of the house, find out how I was gonna get on. Too many pictures staring back at me from a previous time. So I withdrew my remaining 401K, flew coach, saw a lot of people who live worse lives than us, which maybe put things in perspective."

"Where'd you go?"

"Hell, all over. Rio, the Azores, Cameroon, Berlin, Phuket. It's not too bad, financially speaking, when you're traveling alone. Find one of them rental deals online for a shitty house in a shitty part of town, take the buses or cabs to the nicer areas. Hit some beaches. It's all cheap. Except for Europe, the American dollar goes a long way. Shit, a man could live like a king in Africa and Thailand for what we pay minimum wage workers here."

Ray nodded, keeping an eye on the lawn. "I've heard that. Had a friend who taught English in Bangkok years ago. So what did you do? Snorkling? Golf? Museums?"

"I suppose you could call it a spiritual journey. Soul searching. Learned a lot about speaking to higher powers. Don't worry, I'm not a religious nut. I don't even go to church. I just needed some questions answered."

"Tough questions, huh? I can't imagine . . . "

Quinn stared intently into his beer. "Tough indeed.

But I found what I was looking for."

The remaining hour till sunset was filled with small talk, until finally the sun began to dip and Quinn stood up. "Well, none of them traps are springing. The bastards might be waiting till night. They do that sometimes. And lucky for you I'm getting too tired to stick around and wait. Tell you what, I'll come by in the morning and look. If you're up I'll get you."

Quinn shook his new neighbor's hand and smiled. "Deal. And hey, thanks for helping. I really appreciate it. We'll get this lawn looking good yet."

• • •

THE SKY WASHED down in purple hues while Ray made a microwave dinner of Swedish meatballs and pasta. The first of the rain hit the windows around the time the prime time network television shows came on. The picture on the TV became choppy as the weather affected the satellite dish affixed to the side of the house, but Ray didn't care. He threw *Die Hard* into the DVD player and watched John McClain run around in bare feet for the umpteenth time.

By the end of the movie's first act, the rain was hitting the house so hard he thought it might tear the stucco off the house. It was only seconds later the sky blazed white and blue as lightning tore apart the night, followed by a throaty rumble of thunder. "Weird," he muttered. He'd heard thunderstorms were incredibly rare in Southern California. They happened, sure, but you could count the annual thunderstorms on two or three fingers if you were lucky. "Beats a wildfire," he said, aware he was talking out loud to himself. I should really get a dog, he thought. Someone to talk to and maybe even a means of keeping the gophers away.

Boom! The house shook and Ray nearly fell to his knees. "The fuck . . ."

He was sure the house had just been struck by lightning, but what were the odds? The TV turned to static and hissed at him. Then it turned off as the lights flickered and went out. Everything went dark.

"Fucking great."

He moved to the front window and looked across the street at Benito's house. The power was still on over there. So it was true, his house had been hit. Talk about shitty luck. "Of course. Just me."

Before he let the curtains fall back in place he noticed something on his front lawn. It was glowing. Faintly. He almost couldn't be sure, but if he used his peripheral vision he could definitely see the yard pulsing the dimmest orange.

No, not the yard. Just the couple trenches he'd dug. He opened the front door and looked out. The rain pelted him trough the screen door and soaked his face. The trenches shifted to a deeper red, then back to orange. So faint, but it was there.

He raced to the back door and opened it, looked out over the back yard. Here too the trenches showed the faintest glow. Ignoring the rain, he stepped out, was immediately soaked. He moved over the muddy lawn and stared down into the gullies he and Quinn had made. It was as if the earth itself was glowing through the mud. He studied his yard, saw the glowing lines stretching from his fence to the house, saw the ring of red and orange running along the perimeter. It almost looked like . . .

Crash!

Several bolts of lightning stabbed down all around him, exploding up dirt, throwing him to the ground. He thought for sure he was dead, but when he raised his head in the pouring rain, he saw he'd been untouched. It was a miracle.

The hair on his arms was still standing as he got up on his knees and noticed the tiny fires where the lightning had struck.

"The traps," he whispered, realizing the lightning had been attracted to all the gopher traps Quinn had laid. But what were the odds of more than one bolt of lightning striking at once? It was astronomical.

The sky above flashed white for a moment. He knew it wasn't safe outside. With a rush of adrenaline he raced back inside and slid the door shut behind him. He spun and looked out at the backyard with its glowing lines and tiny fires.

And he knew. He knew this wasn't normal. Especially those lines. They seemed to come right up to the back of the house and go underneath. In fact, if he stood tall enough, it looked like . . .

"The fuck . . . ?"

He raced up the stairs to the guest bedroom, threw back the curtains and looked at the front lawn. The glowing lines also now appeared to come right up the front door and go under the house. Across the hall, he stole a glance out the bathroom window overlooking the backyard. The lines weren't random at all. They were linked at points, each of which was on fire. The perimeter ring formed a circle around it all.

I need to get higher, he realized.

In the hall, he yanked down the attic hatch, let the stairs unfold, and climbed up into the insulated, hot tip of the A-frame of the house. He made his way across the rotting beams to the gable vent and gave it a kick, breaking the rusty housing free. Not exactly smart in a thunderstorm, but it was corroded anyway so he may as well replace it. The hole was just big enough to squeeze through, get himself turned around facing upwards, and grab the roof overhang. Carefully, he slid out and up, getting his footing on the roof until he could pull himself up.

The dark purple sky lit up amber again as the bolts of lightning came down. This is beyond stupid, he thought, but he had to know if what he was seeing outside the house was real. He scrambled up the slope and planted one foot on either side of the roof's fold, and swiveled his head, taking in both the front and back yards.

It was a pentagram. They'd dug a fucking pentagram.

He barely had time to question how and why when he heard footsteps behind him. He spun and found himself face to face with a lumbering shadow, clomping toward him, like a drunk linebacker. The lightning flashed again and the shadow lit up. Ray caught sight of something half man and half beast. A black face hiding black orb eyes. A dark purple sneer lined with several rows of tiny, razor sharp piranha-like teeth. Its entire body was covered in dark blue scales and black skin, its legs moved on high hocks like a dog, and some kind of chitin-like wings stretched up over its head. The lightning flashed again as it clomped forward with zeal, and Ray saw it for what it was, some kind of lizard man straight out of a nightmare.

Ray backpedaled, his jaw hanging open, his face now beading with tiny drops of rain. His foot hit the edge of the roof, and without thinking he bent down, swung himself over the side and let his feet find the open gable vent to the attic.

The beast lurched forward, snarling, clawed fingers raking the shingles just as Ray let go and pulled himself inside the attic. His heart slammed against his ribs and his knees wobbled as he tried to rationalize what was going on. But nothing made sense.

Now he heard the distinct buzz of massive wings, rolled over on his back and looked out the vent opening. The beast hovered in the air just outside. Those razor-sharp teeth snapped for good measure.

"Who are you!"

There was no reply as the demon flew to the vent and started to come inside, ducking its head in first then bringing in its arms and legs.

Ray finally found his legs as a wave of adrenaline coursed through him. He leapt up and ran for the attic stairs, jumped past them all and landed in the hallway. He raced toward the main staircase, hearing the footsteps above him, hearing the creature fumbling with the attic ladder. He raced down the stairs and made for the front door, only to find it locked. His fingers fumbled with the latch as the clomping footsteps reached the top of the stairs.

He got the lock open, flung wide the door, and collided with the man standing there in the rain. A baseball bat came out of nowhere and caught him square in the nose, pitching him backwards into his living room. He saw stars, felt blood run from his nostrils. His vision wobbled and he swallowed a tooth. The pain was exquisite, and he wasn't sure he could feel his legs anymore. When he looked up he saw someone standing above him in the darkness. For a beat there was nothing but the sound of rain against the front picture window, then a voice. "Sorry, Ray. I really am. You seem like a nice guy."

"Quinn?"

"Yeah. Sorry. Wasn't trying to hit you that hard. You need to be in good shape for this. But I figured if I just punched you you'd still go right past me.

Ray sat up, rubbing his face. His words were muffled, lost behind a pain he never dreamed possible. But still, there was that other thing clomping around upstairs that looked like it was going to hurt even worse. "Quinn, help me, there's a fucking monster—"

"I know. It's coming."

"We gotta get outta here." Dear God it hurt to talk, he thought.

Quinn's foot came down and caught Ray in the head, knocking him flat to the floor. "Can't let you leave, friend. This is a delicate process."

Ray's head throbbed. He stared at his neighbor

looming above him. Why was he hitting him? What was that thing upstairs? What was going on?

The creature stomped down the stairs, knocking pictures off the wall with its wings. Quinn stepped away from it, shaking. He was scared of it, but not as terrified as he should be. Not as terrified as Ray was.

The beast reached the floor and swung around the balustrade and into the living room. Quinn was up against the wall now. Ray was on the floor, feeling his balls tighten in fear.

"Not me," Quinn said to it. "I called you. You take *him*."

The beast studied Ray, looked back and forth to Quinn a few times, then seemed to realize what part each man played in this situation.

"What the fuck, Quinn?" was all Ray could get out.

Quinn swallowed, relaxing ever so slightly, knowing the beast wasn't going to attack him now. "I did a lot of traveling. Spoke to a lot of interesting people. People that dabbled in things I only dreamed of before. Dark arts. Black magic. It exists, Ray. Oh man does it exist. Took me a while to get all the information I needed. A bit here, a bit there. All over the world. Every culture has ideas on how to make a deal with the devil, you know. I just needed to take bits from each location, piece them together. But shit, I didn't know if it would really work. Figured if nothing else, we'd kill some gophers. But when I saw the storm clouds overhead, and the lightning coming down in your yard, I knew. I knew I'd done it."

"Done what? What does it want?"

With a quick snap, the demon bent down and grabbed Ray by his leg, hauled him up and dangled him in the air like a man caught in a trap. It snarled and licked its lips as Ray swung to and fro.

"Quinn! Make it stop! Please!"

His back still against the wall, Quinn shook his head no. "Can't. Not now. Not when it's working. I need it to work. Should be quick. I hope."

"Quinn!"

"You have no friends here. You won't be missed for a while."

"Quinn! Please!"

"A life for a life, Ray. That's all it boils down to. If nothing else, take solace in the fact you're giving someone else a better life."

New footfalls came down the stairs now, lighter, more tentative. Ray caught sight of a teenage girl in a long summer dress. Her face was blue, bruised and pocked with blood. A gash ran across her neck, exposing her trachea. But as she stepped into the living room, the gore faded from her features, blood drying and flaking off, cuts closing up, her milky white eyes moistening and forming irises of brilliant blue. The scar across her jugular vanished.

"Dad?" she whispered, confused, lost. A tear fell from her eye. "Dad? What . . . ?"

"Quinn! Please!"

"Ray, I need her. I need my baby girl back. It was the only way. It's an even exchange. You understand, right? A body for a body. Christ, Ray, I need her back."

The creature bellowed and grabbed Ray.

"No!" Ray screamed, feeling himself suddenly rising. The ceiling exploded around him as he was flown upwards, through the attic, the roof exploding away, up into the night sky. The earth grew farther away. He felt the air go chill, his body upside down, feet held in a death grip by the demon. The storm danced around him, rain lashing his eyes, lightning stitching past his face. The beast roared, dug its claws into Ray's ankle enough to pierce bone, and changed direction, arcing back down toward the ground, taking Ray with him. With the velocity of a fighter jet it sped back toward earth. The wind whipped through Ray's hair, up his nose, making it difficult to breathe. The ground came up so fast he barely saw it. His stomach lurched into his throat and he could do little but scream and brace for an impact that would surely kill him.

They hit the center of his backyard and pain erupted like white light throughout his body. But he did not die. With half open eyes he saw dirt rush past him, felt the earth go colder as he was dragged down . . . down . . . down, until he could see nothing but darkness and hear nothing except his own muffled cries. And still they went ever downward, that claw around his ankle. Down into the earth.

• • •

Quinn held his daughter close, cooed to her. She was confused and scared and her words were naught but babbles, but her body was warm and she recognized him. That much he could tell. He took her by her hand and walked into the backyard where a giant hole now punctuated the center of the glowing lines. Over the next many seconds the glowing faded, and the hole began to fill in, until finally it was just a shallow divot.

His daughter finally found words. "Dad? Where am I? What's going on?"

Quinn found the nearest gopher trap, still licking with tiny flames. He shook the fire away and looked at the mystical symbol he'd etched into it. This one a glyph he'd uncovered in Poland, taught to him by a blind, mad monk who he found bathing in rodent blood and wearing the severed hand of an unborn baby around his neck.

It actually worked, Quinn thought. Tears rolled down his cheek as he looked at his daughter, her face now a rosy pink.

"What's going on, Dad?"

"Nothing, sweetie. Just killing some gophers. C'mon. Let's go home."

ALSO FROM GRAND MAL PRESS

A SHADOW CAST IN DUST
by Ben Johnson

The ancient order of the web spinners is changing. An old friend returns brandishing a curious silver knife, and Stewart Zanderson is drawn into a strange world of wonder and deceit. The ensuing bloody scene sets Detective Clementine Figgins on his tail, and into a case she could never explain. But the boy, escaped from the dreaded warehouse, now has the knife. And running from his captors through the canyons of San Diego with his new friends and special dog. The ancient order will change, but who will rise when the dust settles?

"An engaging Urban Fantasy Adventure, full of action!"
— Ryan C. Thomas, author of *The Summer I Died*

ALSO FROM GRAND MAL PRESS

The Worst Man on Mars
by Mark Roman & Corben Duke

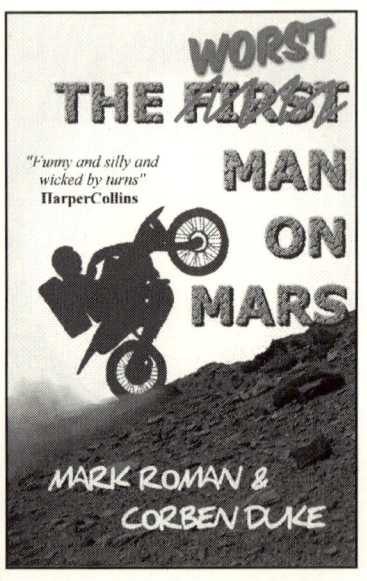

Flint Dugdale, blunt Yorkshireman and reality TV show winner, seems an unlikely contender for First Man on Mars. The Right Stuff he is not. But the tragic death of the mission's brave commander has created a vacancy which Dugdale, with his large frame and 'persuasive personality', has been quick to fill. In charge of a quirky group of British colonists about to land on the Red Planet, and with his place in History assured, Dugdale plans to see out the rest of the mission drinking lager, eating pies and watching his favourite sports on wide-screen TV.

But all is not well on the Martian surface. For five years an advance party of robots with evolving AI personalities have been building Botany Base. They are a long way behind schedule and have made some crucial dimensioning errors. There is Life down there. But will it be pleased to see him?

Available in paperback and ebook formats.

"This is a very enjoyable manuscript. It bounces along, funny and silly and wicked by turns, and fits into a well-established genre which would most definitely find an audience." – HarperCollins Publishers

"Very inventive, imaginative, and funny from cover to cover." – Kevin Bergeron, author of *In a Cat's Eye*

"A brilliantly funny and cleverly conceived work."
– Rob Gregson, author of *Unreliable Histories*

"The funniest sci-fi I've ever read … and I don't even like sci-fi!" – Frank Kusy, author of *Rupee Millionaires*

ALSO FROM GRAND MAL PRESS

"*The Summer I Died* is a tense bloody ride!" - Brian Keene, author of *Pressure*

"*The Summer I Died* will leave a mark on you! This is not a tale you will forget!" - Scream Magazine

"*The Summer I Died* is an endurance test. If you want to freak yourself out on your next camping trip, you can't really do any better." - BloodyDisgusting.com

"*Born to Bleed* is an excellent example of hard-hitting, relentless horror!" - HorrorDrive-in.com

"Ryan C. Thomas absolutely delivers! *Scars of the Broken* is an expertly-crafted mixture of suspense, gore, and humor!" - BMoviesandEbooks.com

www.grandmalpress.com

ALSO FROM GRAND MAL PRESS

DUST OF THE DEVIL'S LAND
by Bryan Killian

It only took a matter of days for the zombies to overrun Redding, California. Those unlucky enough to survive prayed for salvation at the hands of the military only to find new horrors awaiting them. Two boys, riding out the end of the world in a tree house, are now faced with eventual starvation unless they venture beyond streets of their once idyllic neighborhood. Not an easy situation to be in when you can't trust adults. Pockets of survivors huddle together to form what's left of humanity, not knowing a new threat is clawing its way near. Even the strongest survivors can fall to the teeth and claws of the dead. *Dust of the Devil's Land*, Bryan Killian's follow up to Welcome to Necropolis, explores the agony of loss, the will to survive, and the fight to reclaim humanity. Take a wild ride to the final minutes of all we know.

"Killian does a masterful job!"
-Brian Keene, author of *The Rising*

For more Grand Mal Press titles please visit us online at www.grandmalpress.com

Word of mouth is crucial for any author to succeed. If you enjoyed this book, please consider leaving a review on Amazon or Goodreads. Even a couple sentences can make a world of difference and is very much appreciated. Thank you for reading!